Iced Tea at Gelson's

A Spiritual Memoir of Simple Pleasures

Recipes Included

By Lynda Zussman

Iced Tea at Gelson's
© 2023 Lynda Zussman
Published February 2023 by Lynda Zussman

The coffee bar patrons in this book are fictional characters who represent an amalgam of personality types I have encountered there.

Please consult with your doctor regarding the consumption of any tea. All teas can have side effects and this book is not intended to offer medical advice. Certain teas can interact with supplements or medications; caution is advised.

ISBN: 979-8-218-13624-6

Contact the author at: *zussman28@gmail.com*

The Library of Congress has cataloged this edition as follows:
Name: Zussman, Lynda, author.

Cover image purchased from Canva

Interior layout and cover compilation by Alane Pearce, Pearce Writing Services LLC contact: apearcewriting@gmail.com

ABOUT THE AUTHOR

Lynda Zussman is the author of *Throw Me the Rope: A Memoir on Loving Lauren*. An excerpt from her book was published in the Los Angeles Times. With a background in education, Lynda has worked as a writer, consultant, advocate, and speaker. She conducts journal writing workshops and presentations for teens and adults to help them discover their authentic selves. During her time in three different school districts, she focused on developing students' self-esteem and diverse style of learning. Lynda has authored two screenplays, *Panic* and *Papa Rose*, and both were optioned for TV and film. Lynda served as co-anchor for the national TV show *Financial Inquiry*. Lynda lives in Austin, enjoying her family and her dog, Cowboy.

For Ashlie

"i carry your heart
(i carry it in my heart)"
e. e. cummings

"The only journey is the one within."

Rainer Maria Rilke

TABLE OF CONTENTS

RECIPES

ICED TEA AT GELSON'S

A SPIRITUAL MEMOIR OF SIMPLE PLEASURES

LYNDA ZUSSMAN

INTRODUCTION

In this world of aging, death, and persistent chaos, the ritual of tea can bring enlightenment and peace. Disappointments, challenges, and stressful events are a part of life, but it is how we respond that makes all the difference. If you have a base of strong principles, you can create powerful solutions to survive almost anything. In this world of chaos, pandemics, and loss, we seek moments of calm, comfort, or solace. The ritual of tea can bring enlightenment, wisdom, and peace.

Author Lynda Zussman survived the infamous 1980 MGM Las Vegas fire and the loss of her adult daughter in 2008. To keep moving forward, she embraces the ritual of tea and allows herself time and space to process. She shows us how we must take our circumstances and find the solution to craft a productive and creative lifestyle. We must make "The Choice" of how we want life to be, regardless of our past and present life. The future is ours to create; this memoir covers it all with real life situations and concrete solutions.

With a backdrop of the simple pleasure of iced tea, Lynda employs humor and charm to take you on a journey of resilience. She ponders the weighty life-and-death issues and gives the same attention to modest delights like her own favorite recipes. Although she lived in places like Newport Beach, Bel Air with its movie stars, and the mountain town of Calabasas (before The Kardashians), the daily ritual of *Iced Tea at Gelson's* became her oasis.

Socialization, familiar rituals, and simple pleasures are keys to a long, productive, happy life. With its display of grit, tenacity, and perseverance, this book will stay with you for a long time; you may find yourself returning to it often for insightful tips toward a more integrated lifestyle and a path to celebrating your own unique human spirit.

CHAPTER 1

FINDING MY ANCHOR

"The secret of life is enjoying the passage of time."

— *James Taylor*

Food! Glorious food! Some people eat to live; some people live to eat. I am somewhere in the middle, but surely a foodie. I believe that a good life includes sharing delicious meals with family and friends, going to a restaurant for a culinary feast, and frequent visits to a gourmet grocery store. Food and drink are companions to not only our celebrations, but also our times of sadness. We find comfort in the familiar rituals of eating and drinking.

One enduring theme of my life is the ritual of tea, particularly at Gelson's coffee bar. Almost anyone who has spent time in Southern California knows Gelson's Markets. Since my twenties, their unique coffee bars have served as my second home. When I walk into Gelson's, a half-dozen neighbors or employees greet me and call me by name. I am home. Gelson's is a place where I align myself with myself. It doesn't matter if it's hot tea or iced tea; the experience leads me to a state of peace.

The Gelson's Brothers empire was created with devotion, creativity, and perseverance. Long before the Costco days. Bernard and Eugene Gelson began helping their father's Iowa Grocery store. As adults, they developed a vision of bringing quality goods to the public and creating a shopping experience that would bring customers back again and again. They were on to something.

After World War II, the Gelson brothers moved to California and opened the first Gelson's Market in Burbank in 1951, the year I was born. The Arden Group Managed Gelson's from 1966 until 2014, when they sold Gelson's to TPG Capital, a billion-dollar company. As of today, the Pan Pacific International Holdings has acquired the Gelson's Supermarket.

Known for their exceptional cleanliness, superior customer service, and superb quality of fresh food, Gelson's was recently selected as number one of the premier supermarkets in Southern California, and they keep improving. Offering gourmet prepared meals, local organic produce, and a superior beer and wine selection, Gelson's is Southern California upscale haven for specialty foods. And this is where my tea addiction all started.

My personal journey has been both exhilarating and devastating. The highs and the lows pile up over the decades: a loving mother, a difficult father, a lost job, a cross-country move, a whirlwind romance, a budding new career, a spate of panic attacks, two beautiful daughters, a terrifying fire, a dream home, the death of a loved one, the birth of grandchildren. Through all of this, the ritual of tea has served as my bedrock for healing, enlightenment, wisdom, and peace.

Buddhist principles warn us about having an unsettled "monkey mind" that keeps us from peace and serenity. My daily ritual of iced tea at Gelson's has helped me on the path to living with authenticity and intention; the pause of enjoyment promotes self-compassion for dealing with our own issues, and this leads us to have compassion for others. We're made with two hands – one hand to take care of ourselves, and the other to help those in need.

We seek a more perfect state of being through maintaining relationships with others, connecting to beauty of all forms, and embracing rituals like a simple cup of tea. Tea is my daily regimen regardless of my state of mind. Sometimes I want to be alone and simply be present; sometimes I need socialization to combat depression, anxiety, and loneliness. I came to rely on the company of friends and strangers at Gelson's. With a regular cast of distinct personalities, the coffee bar reminds me of some well-known sitcom ensembles like those in *Cheers* or *Friends*. It's a place for camaraderie, peace, serenity, and stability in a chaotic world. The social atmosphere there is organically integrated with the pleasures of the tea ritual.

Gelson's Market stirs up a lot of my childhood memories about food. In my family, food was love. My mom made a ritual of delicious meals that brought our chaotic family together every day. I have indelible memories of her specialties like crispy fried chicken, homemade spaghetti sauce, juicy steak, and rustic potato salad. Summertime in Chicago meant that the farmer's market had red ripe beefsteak tomatoes and fresh-shucked corn that was a meal in itself. And the desserts! When I remember the delight of Mom's cherry chocolate cake, I salivate like Pavlov's dog. She loved to feed her family and the neighborhood kids.

When I left Chicago behind, I discovered Gelson's in California. Gelson's was my healthy addiction. A day was not complete until I had my Paradise tropical iced tea from the coffee bar. I would muddle through each day, good or bad, to get to my moment of peace at Gelson's. Some people drink at bars; some go to daily AA meetings; some go to their yoga, Pilates, or meditation classes. There are mahjong players, bridge players, and knitting classes for people who are social animals. For my own social purposes, I go to Gelson's.

Tea is my ritual, and Gelson's became my anchor for that. I might meet friends for a chat, have a business meeting, bump into a neighbor, or simply enjoy my tea alone. I have been a regular at several different Gelson's stores, because we moved around Southern California quite a bit. No matter which store, the coffee bar was a safe harbor, always my oasis no matter what was going on in my life. I have experienced my joys, triumphs, and tragedies by always having a place to recharge or just enjoy the simple pleasure of drinking an iced tea.

The tea ritual always brings me to a sense of harmony. I can feel my shoulders soften as my body relaxes and my breath returns to a regular rhythm. When I take that first sip of iced tea, I sense a chemical change in my body. The taste is satisfying and crisp. I get a zap of energy, unlike my coffee jolt in the morning, and yet I also feel a sense of calm.

On some levels, I believe the comfort that I experience during my tea ritual relates to the safety of my childhood. The fundamental pleasure of tea and the camaraderie at the coffee bar recall simpler times and the tightly knit community of my midwestern roots. It's as comforting as a bowl of home-made granola.

HOME MADE GRANOLA

INGREDIENTS
- 5 cups old-fashioned oats
- 1 cup of brown sugar
- 1 cup flaked coconut
- 1 tbsp ground cinnamon
- 1 tsp ground nutmeg
- 1/2 cup water
- 1/2 cup vegetable oil
- 1 tbsp vanilla extract
- 1/2 dried cranberries
- 1/2 cup sliced or slivered almonds or chopped walnuts

DIRECTIONS
- Preheat oven to 325 degrees F
- Mix oats, brown sugar, coconut, cinnamon, and nutmeg together in a large bowl. Stir water, oil, and

vanilla extract into the oat mixture: spread onto a baking sheet
- Bake in preheated oven, stirring every 15 minutes

until golden brown and crunchy, about 1 hour
- Transfer to a bowl, stir cranberries and almonds

through the granola. Enjoy with tea

CHAPTER 2

CHICAGO

"Would you like an adventure now,
or shall we have our tea first?"
— *Peter Pan*

I grew up on the South Side of Chicago during the 50s and 60s. The neighborhood known as Jeffrey Manor was part of the postwar housing boom, fueling the residential growth of the southeast side of Chicago. The curvy streets completed loops with clusters of homes. The duplexes and single-family homes that lined the streets gave Jeffrey Manor a suburban feel right in the middle of the city.

We lived in a new development with cookie-cutter tract housing. The school and grocery store were within blocks of our home. The neighbors never locked their doors, and the kids were always playing up and down the streets. The lilac-colored Magnolia trees were in full glorious bloom during spring and summer. The neighborhood children would hang from the branches with scuffed knees and dirty clothes. The fireflies, rich in their ruby and black hues, were chased by children of all ages. We never went home until it was dark outside, and no one was checking on us to see if we have been kidnapped.

During the summer we went to Rainbow Beach and Summer Camp. I remember my mother sending me to the Sulie-Harand Children's Art School when I was ten years old. A yellow bus would pick me up and drive a dozen pre-teens downtown. We had three classes on Saturday mornings: dance, singing, and acting.

My father owned a metalworks shop named Brown Metal Spinning, where he contracted to do a lot of work for US Steel. I remember his marketing slogan: *If We Can't Do It, Forget It.* He also made the base for the famous lava lamps. We had a different colored lava lamp in each of our rooms. It was a prosperous business, and he was a good provider. My dad came home after a ten-hour day, often arriving with dirty hands and soiled clothes, but it was reliable work that fed five people in our house.

My dad employed a half-dozen hard working men and my brother worked there with his friends, sometimes during the summer. In his early twenties, Dad had been a middleweight professional boxer who fought at Madison Square Garden and won a Golden Gloves Award in the 1930s. But it was my father's family business that thrived during my childhood years. We owned our three-bedroom house with a lovely yard and food was on the table. Life was good.

During my teen years, I did not have much of a relationship with him. We seemed to go our separate ways. I do remember, however, the salami, onion, tomato, and ketchup sandwiches on white bread that he would whip up for us. Food in the kitchen was a key center place for all of us.

My dad golfed with his buddies on Wednesdays and played gin rummy one night a week. Kosher deli food was laid out for the men to eat at each of their houses. My father worked very hard, sometimes six days a week, enjoying his new black Cadillac.

We had a housekeeper, Lucille, who came on Fridays; often, she drank our liquor and then tried to hide the fact by refilling the bottles with water. My mom did not mind, because she was too good and too nice to fire. I loved Lucille as I watched her iron our clothes meticulously, with a cigarette dangling from her lips. She always made me feel special when I would visit with her while she did her chores.

Mom would prepare canned salmon with onions and vinegar for Lucille, and I would maybe have a Swanson TV dinner. I felt then (and now) that you can't beat the roasted turkey, string beans, mashed potatoes, and a petite brownie for dessert. It was like getting a prize in the Cracker Jack box.

We often flew to Miami and vacationed there during the freezing winters. However, we were very middle-class, enjoying the benefits of the rising economy. Just blocks away were the bigger, more expensive houses in a neighborhood known as Pill Hill. Pill Hill was the kind of neighborhood preferred by professionals like lawyers and doctors drawn to the homes with circular driveways and multiple bathrooms.

Not long ago, someone tried to assess my early years by asking how many bathrooms we had when we lived in Chicago. My answer was perhaps misleading. Although the house came with just one bathroom, my father built two more – one in the attic and one in the basement. A resourceful man, he also built our garage, even though the resulting structure was slightly lopsided.

My dad was strict, quiet, and moody. However, he was a very involved parent when I was a small child. He often took me to Kiddy Land on Sundays after he watched baseball on TV. I would go on the Ferris wheel or the roller coaster. I also often went for pony rides, and then topped it off with pink cotton candy.

On birthdays, he would ring the doorbell and would hide to surprise me with a gift. On my seventh birthday, I was greeted with an infamous 36-inch Chatty Cathy doll. I have a vivid memory of another birthday when he gave me a shiny new bicycle.

One holiday season, he took me to the five and dime store and asked me which toy doll I liked. We looked at the porcelain dolls at the top of the shelves with colorful clothes and animated faces. I pointed to a half dozen dolls while a salesperson inconspicuously followed behind us. All of them appeared on our sofa one Christmas/Hanukkah morning! He was full of surprises and often brought toys home after work. It was often a Santa Claus vs. a Mr. Hyde moment.

However, he taught me how to swim, ride a bike, and drive a car, but his rage always made the home uneasy. He fought with my mother constantly. Perhaps the boxing had caused a brain injury that led to his erratic behavior, or perhaps he had an undiagnosed condition. I was fearful of this man and to this day, he is an enigma.

He did have a sense of humor, certainly with his buddies. Dad would upstage the entertainment at Bar Mitzvahs and weddings by taking over the microphone and cracking his own jokes that amused everyone. He frequently answered our phone at home with "Brown's Summer Home; some are home, some are not." Yes, Dad was a deep, sometimes troubled man with many faces. From what I was told, his childhood was no picnic.

My brother, Roger, was my hero. We often played together even though he was four years older than me. One game we called "horse," by which he would tie a rope around my neck and walk me through the house. We watched *Captain Kangaroo, Roy Rogers & Dale Evans,* and *Howdy Doody.* Prior to Halloween, my father took us to a seamstress who made Roy Rogers and Dale Evans costumes for us. He did love us as children, but he was cold and distant when we were teens. I never had a meaningful conversation with him. I remember one Thanksgiving Day when my father screamed incessantly; we ended up eating our turkey, mashed potatoes, and fixings in each of our rooms. That kind of tension had a special place in our home and would visit us often. When he died, I had a lot of unresolved anger to work through.

After dinner, our neighbors sat outside lounging on our front lawn, smoking cigarettes. My mom enjoyed her role as a home-maker and mother – cleaning, cooking, and taking care of the family. Life was very simple back then. She had a quiet demean-or and was accepting of life and her marriage, although I am sure there were times when she felt trapped.

I accompanied my mother to our grocery store, *The National,* almost every day. She would push her metal buggy cart and, if I were lucky, I would get a coloring book and a box of Raisinets. Mother was a very attractive platinum blonde; a fit model for Spiegel's Catalogue in her twenties who was perfectly happy being a stay-at-home housewife, raising three kids. Wearing June Cleaver dresses and Zsa Zsa Gabor pearls, she elicited a respect-ful admiration from the men in the meat market, who would scramble for her attention.

My mom would often toss steak and iceberg lettuce in her cart for the evening dinner. As we exited the small strip mall, we passed the cleaners, the bakery, the dress shop, the shoe store, the five and dime store, the drug store, and the bowling alley that had the best little greasy spoon restaurant attached. There was even a small medical building behind the drug store, making it conve-nient for those who did not drive, such as my mother.

At the bowling alley restaurant, I would often order a small steak meal for lunch with my mother after grocery shopping. One early evening, my parents were going to a wedding and my mom gave me the $1.25 for my typical steak dinner. I was close to ten years old, and I was allowed to go alone. I ordered the steak dinner, but I received a huge steak with all the fixings. When I received a bill for $5.95, I didn't know what to do. My parents were not home, and I did not have the money. I told the owner of the restaurant I would go home and get the money. I gathered all the coke bottles and turned them in for cash at the grocery store, and earned enough to pay the bill. I'm still proud of that tender-age problem solving attitude.

In our neighborhood, we were visited frequently by a vegetable truck, a candy truck, and the Good Humor man. The vegetables were farm-fresh, and of course the penny candy and the Good Humor ice cream (announced by the familiar jingle bell) were extremely popular.

In summertime, the municipal mosquito control truck would go up and down our streets spraying DDT; all the kids, including me, would recklessly run through the clouds of smoke billowing out of the back of the truck. At eight years old, I once passed out after running through the smoke. Someone summoned my father and the next thing I knew, my dad was carrying me on his shoulder back home. He was my hero at times, but often my enemy. I was conditioned to be the good little girl, but at the same time the message of not being "good enough" became part of my psyche. Therapy does wonders for the negative messages in childhood and then these messages need to be processed and released.

On the other hand, my mother was soft and gentle, and she emphasized elegance and good manners. I thought she was beautiful. When I was five years old, my mother told me I would one day need a nose job. I only had a slight bump on my nose, but she was into perfection. I remember telling my first-grade teacher that I needed a nose job, not exactly knowing what that was about. But since my classmate Johnny needed knee surgery, I felt free to share my surgical "needs."

Delicious dinners always graced our table. Mom didn't socialize much beyond visiting a couple of neighbors, and she never joined social groups. Our neighbor Faby was an Italian immigrant who came to the US when her German husband (who had immigrated first) brought her over as his bride. They were best friends and would often sit on the front lawn, laughing away with a cigarette or soft drink. Faby's meatballs, made with a recipe from the old country, were unrivaled. The secret ingredient in her tomato sauce was sugar; just enough to bring out the delicious flavor of the garlic and oregano.

Roger and I went to Luella Grammar School, and I recently asked him if he thinks we had ADHD because of our lack of attention in the classroom during those days. He replied by saying it seemed like everyone at Luella had ADHD. The school was just four blocks from my house and my brother walked me to school and back.

My parents never stressed academics. They left it up to us to be responsible. At school I drifted in and out of attentiveness during the oral lessons. I remember how school could be boring, and perhaps that is why I became a dedicated teacher. I think I sometimes disassociated from my environment due to the tension in my home.

Being the third child in the home, I was not overly nurtured; however, I was sheltered, well-fed, and well-dressed. It's hard to pay forward those you didn't have while growing up unless you make a conscious and determined effort to change your mentoring and parenting skills. My mom was always kind to me, and food was her way of giving love. I also had an older sister who is thirteen-years my senior. She left the house when I was five years old. I don't remember her very much except she lived in the remodeled bedroom upstairs. Today we are very close. I think it is pretty obvious that I was an oops baby.

After grammar school, I attended Bowen High School. The South Side has a bad reputation due to the violence that has taken place since I left. In 1966, the infamous Richard Speck committed the heinous crime of torturing, raping, and killing several student nurses, just blocks from my home. This was ground-breaking and made national news, largely because it had been such a quiet, safe community. Despite the hardships there, it was fertile ground for future success. Fellow South Siders include the actor Mandy Patinkin and personal finance guru Suze Orman.

One man on our street had a beautiful, young daughter who died of a brain tumor. He was like the walking dead after that horrific tragedy. A father of my classmate hanged himself in the garage while a brother of another friend died from a gunshot wound. One neighbor disappeared from her family overnight because she was pregnant; unwed mothers were regarded as shameful during that era. Still, in the larger view, life had a flow of safety and security. No one moved away and no one got a divorce. All our neighbors knew each other, even blocks away.

Mrs. Seltzer, my high school counselor, told me to forget about college because I was "too social" and I had very average test scores. Nevertheless, I attended the University of Illinois and graduated from Southern Illinois University. I wanted to be a teacher, and I succeeded. After moving to Southern California, I enrolled at the University of California - Irvine and concentrated in Special Education. I always had a love for teaching; Mrs. Seltzer was wrong. Students with educational, psychological, or social challenges were my passion.

I moved to the Chicago North Side after college and enjoyed the independence of having an apartment and job. It was the seventies, and it was a groovy time. The Gold Coast, Old Town, Michigan Avenue, and the beat of the city were intoxicating. Suburban husbands (sometimes divorced, sometimes not) would leave their families to party hard. Birth control pills were dispensed like Pez candy and the disco clubs were in full operation. Everyone had *Saturday Night Fever.*

When Mary Tyler Moore died in 2017, it brought up a lot of feelings and memories about single women during the seventies. Women's lib was brewing with feminists such as Betty Friedan, Gloria Steinem, and even Marlo Thomas in the forefront; landing a job and an apartment made independent living a gift. Marlo's character in the TV show *That Girl* never slept with her boyfriend; the show was squeaky clean but not so realistic. What did Donald do for sex?

We all read Cosmopolitan Magazine because its naughty editor, Helen Gurley Brown, took feminine sexuality and pleasure to another level. The pill gave women more freedom than ever. The sexual revolution finally began to bring the sexes closer together, slowly diminishing the double standard.

These were the days before venereal diseases were fatal; no one knew about AIDS yet. Too many men wanted women to appear chaste and conservative, while paradoxically ready for fast and easy sex. As Tom Cruise later said in the movie *Cocktail*, "We wouldn't want them to just lay on the ground and throw their legs up in the air."

Women who gave in to first date sex, at least back then, often discovered that they would never see their date again. The lesson endures; sometimes what comes easy isn't worth pursuing. The tension and the buildup of romance almost always prevails, even today. Emotions escalate to that magic moment. Of course, there are exceptions; friends have spoken of vacation sex with one-night stands that were magical, but not sustaining.

A wise woman once shared the axiom that "women who hang out at truck stops pickup truck drivers." This isn't meant to demean all the honorable truck drivers out there, but her message was "don't cheapen yourself." Don't hang out at bars for cheap/easy sex, and she had a point.

It's nice for both sexes today to have a moral compass, especially with the *Me-Too* movement. Sex can be misused, abused, or cherished. It is the ultimate of soul-giving. Intimacy, at its best, can be among the most joyous moments in life. Realistic expectations are important, because it is rarely consistent; life just happens, and romance will ebb and flow.

I did love being an independent single woman in the Windy City. My first apartment in Chicago was just off Lake Shore Drive, a studio apartment for $160 per month. If you stood on your tippy-toes and tilted your head to the right, you could see Lake Michigan between two buildings.

I immediately bought a rattan love seat and a chair from Marshall Fields. There was one Crate & Barrel on Michigan Avenue and one store in Old Town. Shopping or browsing there was my favorite thing to do on a Saturday morning. It was a visual paradise for the eyes and for the foodies. I bought the bulk of my furnishings from Crate & Barrel (founded in Chicago in 1962) and everything was orange.

Orange cushions, orange pillows, and two orange director's chairs adorned my apartment. My father built a long parsons table; I rolled my bed under it and placed two orange bolster pillows against the table to make a day bed, with a colorful madras print spread on top. A butcher block table and a shag rug in the middle of the room made my place delightful and cozy. This was home.

It was a hot June during my first week after moving in, and I needed to hunt for a summer job before I could substitute teach in the fall. I circled many open positions in the newspaper want ads and took the bus down Michigan Avenue. There were many ad-men agencies, stock brokerage houses, and of course the Merchandise Mart. On one sweltering day I interviewed for ten jobs, some of them promising. However, when I got home, I realized I had given out the wrong number for my new landline phone. In a dyslexic moment, I had switched two numbers around. So I turned on the air conditioner, changed out of my interview clothes, and made myself a comforting dinner. At that point, I could not even remember who I contacted.

DINNER FOR A TRAIN WRECK DAY: SIMPLE PASTA
(Wine Included)

INGREDIENTS
- 1/2 lb. of angel hair pasta or your favorite pasta
- 1 cup diced tomatoes, canned or fresh Roma tomatoes
- 1/4 cup olive oil
- 1 tsp oregano
- Dash of red pepper flakes
- 1/8 cup capers
- 2 cloves of garlic, minced
- 1/4 cup curly parsley
- Parmesan cheese

DIRECTIONS
- Boil the pasta until tender, then drain
- Add the olive oil to a large pan; sauté the garlic and add the remaining ingredients except the parsley and cheese
- Cook until dish is blended, then pour over hot pasta
- Add the grated cheese and parsley on top and enjoy
- Don't forget the wine with dinner

Treasure Island was one of the first gourmet grocery stores in Chicago. The Gold Coast affluent crowd shopped there in their mink coats, fancy jewelry, and bouffant hairdos. In my jeans and Gap t-shirts, I shopped there because I was already a foodie. I would rather spend my money on groceries than a trinket on Michigan Avenue. There were no farm markets in my neighborhood, so on Saturday at Treasure Island I would load my car up for the week. Salad makings, soup ingredients, and sandwiches for work would be at the top of my list. I kept all the basic staples in my pantry: pasta, canned tuna, beans, eggs, and Parmesan cheese.

I landed a job at Weiss Memorial Hospital as the girl at the front desk issuing visitor passes. I also connected incoming calls to the patients. There were many nice Jewish women who volunteered at the hospital and sat with me greeting the visitors. They often wanted to fix me up with their nice Jewish relative.

I began dating the head of personnel, a blonde handsome Swedish man. Steve was very shy and told me not to tell anyone we were dating. Steve was Catholic and I was Jewish; I know he was religious, but our different backgrounds weren't a problem for me. He once made a joke about matzo ball soup.

He was very pleasant, but it ultimately went nowhere. We went out on six dates, including a steak dinner at his apartment. He never kissed me good night or made a move on me. It felt so strange because I had such a crush on him. I never figured out why there was no chemistry from his side.

In the fall, I started substitute teaching. No permanent positions were available because every (as it seemed) Jewish girl in Chicago had become a teacher. I was called many times to sub at the John C. Coonley School, and it eventually turned into a permanent position for the year. It was a blue-collar working-class neighborhood with a melting pot population.

I was delighted to have the opportunity to teach the sixth-grade class that no one wanted because of the behavior problems. Half of the class members were special education students. I loved every day and never had a serious problem. I became fully engaged with the students, and the principal kept me on for three more years after I had proved myself.

The special education students constructed a wall mural about Italy, and it was outstanding. With no internet in the seventies, the students did their research with an encyclopedia. They studied and discussed topics like Italian architecture, art, government, history, agriculture, and culture, and then they transferred their notes into drawings.

The other half of the class studied the topic in a more traditional way; they read the assignment from the book and then answered the questions at the end of the chapter. The special education students learned more from creating the wall mural than did those who had read the book, because they had a hands-on multi-sensory experience. I remember the Italian luncheon we arranged with invitations for their parents to see this outstanding piece of work. I did love teaching. I still remember what we assembled for that memorable sixth grade Italian Luncheon.

ITALIAN FARM SALAD

INGREDIENTS
- Roughly equal amounts of salami, provolone cheese, green olives, tomatoes, red onion, cucumber, roasted peppers
- Oregano vinaigrette (olive oil, vinegar, dried oregano)
- Grated Parmesan cheese (optional)

DIRECTIONS
- Combine all ingredients
- Layer over chopped romaine lettuce
- Top with grated cheese

FABY'S MEATBALLS

INGREDIENTS
- 1 tbsp butter
- 3/4 cup minced white onion
- 2 tbsp minced garlic
- 1tsp each salt, pepper, cayenne pepper, nutmeg, oregano, and cumin
- 1 large egg
- 1/4 cup ketchup or Heinz chili sauce
- 1 lb. ground beef
- 1/2 lb. ground pork
- 1/4 cup breadcrumbs

DIRECTIONS
- Preheat oven to 350 degrees F
- Heat butter in large skillet
- Add onion and garlic; stir for ten minutes and let cool
- In a large mixing bowl combine all spices and egg; mix well
- Add ground beef, pork, breadcrumbs, and vegetable mixture
- Add ketchup or chili sauce
- Mix well and make into two-inch balls
- Place meatballs on large oven pan and bake for 30 minutes
- Serve with al dente spaghetti and Rao's jarred tomato sauce

A pitcher of cold iced tea works best with this meal

CHAPTER 3

LOS ANGELES

"In Britain, a cup of tea is the answer to every problem."
— *David Williams*

In 1977, shortly after college, I moved to Los Angeles large-ly because of Chicago's difficult weather and an undesirable teaching assignment. I had lost my prior teaching assignment after three years due to the transfer of new teachers. I also lost my great apartment because of a conversion to condominiums; on top of that, I broke up with my boyfriend. I had no job, no apartment, no boyfriend.

After having a mild nervous breakdown, I worked as a waitress at the swanky *Mel Markons* in Lincoln Park for six months. My fellow waitresses were hot girls who got big tips. I was a horrible waitress who carried a cup in one hand and the saucer in the other, while the experienced servers carried three plates on their arm. I would ineptly deliver the salad for dessert. Somehow, I made more money waitressing than I did teaching, but it was time to make a change.

Go west, young girl, go west. I knew a couple of people in Los Angeles, and I had relatives there. Why not? While still teaching in Chicago, I vacationed at a natural health spa in Guadalajara where I met Stephanie. She was an amazing Bohemian artist who was also an art teacher in a Los Angeles progressive school. Stephanie encouraged me to make the move to California when the time was right.

She was my immediate contact person when I arrived, and she helped me get an apartment. We became good friends, and her funky LA style enthralled me. She owned an art gallery on Melrose Avenue, and we would hang out there for hours. Friends would stop by, and it became my social circle.

A gold Toyota packed with my things brought me to the golden state and a first-grade teaching position. The famous Farmers Market on Third and Fairfax was a daily routine for sharing a cappuccino with friends and grabbing some produce before running off to work. Buying fresh peanut butter was a treat back then because of its novelty, and the homemade crepes were delicious.

The CBS studio was behind the Farmers Market and occasionally I would see a movie star or a celebrity. Many of the locals were there every morning. Some were aspiring actors or writers, waiting to be discovered or make a contact. With its unique vendors, the Farmers Market remains a one-of-a-kind venue.

I dated a lot the first year of living on the west side. I had another great apartment and I really enjoyed teaching. After watching the movie *Looking for Mr. Goodbar* with Diane Keaton (in which she is murdered by someone she had dated), I became very careful, meeting first dates at a local coffee shop or restaurant. Around the same time, the infamous Hillside Strangler had killed many single girls. Some of his victims were prostitutes, but I did wonder if any were teachers.

I hung out with my friends at restaurants and bars like *Joe Allen*, *The Daisy*, *The Saloon*, and *Pips*, the private club. Two of my close friends worked to provide catered meals to the homes of movie stars and to their parties. I was invited to many of the parties where I would sit in the kitchen, chatting with my friends.

Soleil Moon, who went on to play Punky Brewster, was often in my arms as an infant while her mother Sondra and Stephanie dished out the food. They were both incredible chefs who also catered on movie sets. Their *Off the Wall Catering* business was very prosperous in those days before Wolfgang Puck. I could not fail to notice that the homes in Bel Air and Beverly Hills were spectacular, too. This was not Chicago.

I was on a pristine sandy shoreline at Marina del Rey beach in 1978 when I met my husband David, twelve months after arriving in LA. It was a Sunday at the end of April, one month before our Memorial Day elopement. Sounds ridiculous, right? Who would marry anyone in one month?

New to Los Angeles, I was teaching and very comfortable in my brand-new apartment. Dating, however, had been a culture shock. Everyone moved so fast, and I was taking a break from dating. In one month, I dated a conceited Malibu doctor, an actor on *General Hospital* (waitresses kept asking for his autograph), and an author who became famous for writing books on screenwriting.

I later met up with a couple of girlfriends from college who quickly connected me to the parties, bars, and 70s drug culture. It was a time of sex, drugs, and rock and roll. I was clean and sober from the beginning because drugs were never part of my playground. I felt the shift from good clean mid-western living to a jaded but exciting and entertaining world.

I hung out with friends, nested in my apartment, and spent Saturdays at the deli, Nate n' Als, or the movies. Cooking was something that remained a passion; suddenly I enjoyed being single and taking a break from dating.

On one glorious sunny day, I went to the beach with a friend who was visiting from Chicago. Sunbathing on our blanket, we were next to a group of boisterous young men who were drinking beer and playing football. I thought of them as "the players" when they approached our blanket, one by one, attempting to score. Today, they might better be labeled the "booty call boys." They were crude, obnoxious, and unwelcome. I recall that one had a poorly executed corn weave hair line. We sent each one away.

And then suddenly, a handsome gentleman tumbled onto my blanket while trying to catch a football. *Handsome.* He had a calm, suave, self-assured demeanor.

"Look," he said, with dark piercing eyes and a killer smile, "I don't want to bother you. I know my buddies are giving you and your friend a hard time, but here is my business card and I would really like to have lunch with you. I heard that you don't give out your phone number." (No, not since Diane Keaton's character was murdered and the Hillside Strangler was still on the loose.)

We chatted briefly, and that was the extent of our encounter that sunny day. As we were leaving, I glanced back to see this hunk of a man throw the football to his friend and I paused with a bit of awe.

A few days later, I called "Handsome" and I quickly identified myself as the girl on the blanket at the beach who does not give out her phone number. He countered with "But you do eat dinner." With that, we made a date.

I donned my shiny pink jeans which I regarded as my magical pants. Boy, would I love to be able to fit into those pants today. Of course, Handsome drove a white Corvette, the automotive equivalent to a white horse. He was trouble! He was a man who could capture and break your heart in a minute.

We dined at a cafe on Melrose Avenue, and it felt like we were on a ride. By thirty-five it was clear to me that he was a playboy. During dinner I told him that I would never get involved with someone like him, let alone marry a womanizer.

We then went to an upscale nightclub with disco music (yes, *Saturday Night Fever* style) in The Blue Whale Design Center. We were caught up in the joy of the music, the glamorous setting, and the escalating physical attraction for each other. It was dangerous, magnetic, and so very tempting.

I felt like we were Tony and Maria from *West Side Story* in the auditorium, that no one else was in the room. We sat very close to each other after dancing (yes, Handsome can dance too) when the inevitable kiss happened. I was romantically drunk, but I stuck to my principles. I said goodnight at the end of the evening with no expectations of another date.

Handsome then called me when he got home and said I was in the driver's seat. I hung up on him not believing a word he said, but eventually a second and third date followed. Finally, I had to take charge and I appeared at the door wearing nothing but a terrycloth robe. I dropped the robe. It was time to surrender, but I maintained an element of control by calling the initial shot of "come and get it." From that day on, we were inseparable.

I soldiered on as a dedicated teacher, even as I was coming into my classroom that last month of the school year frequently hung over from our champagne parties and disco dancing. Just the two of us, up until three in the morning, having a good time. It was a manic month of romantic craziness. My friends who knew him warned me about this playboy, but every coin has two sides.

I took a chance and found out this man had genuine qualities of loyalty, kindness, and integrity. We eloped to Las Vegas exactly 28 days from our first date. Never wavering, we've endured a life of raising two beautiful daughters and a forty-year marriage. We make a good team. As my grandma use to say, "Every cup has a saucer."

HEALTHY EASY MUFFINS

INGREDIENTS
- 2 1/4 cups oat bran or oatmeal
- 1 tsp baking soda
- 1/4 cup pure maple syrup
- Handful of raisins or dried blueberries (chocolate chips optional)
- 1 1/4 cup milk
- 1 egg
- 2 ripe bananas

DIRECTIONS
- Preheat oven to 350 degrees F
- Combine dry with wet ingredients
- Spray muffin tin with nonstick spray (olive oil)
- Fill cups 2/3 full; bake for 25 minutes or until firm
- Serve with chai tea

CHAPTER 4

NEWPORT BEACH (THE FIRST TIME)

"Tea to the English is really a picnic indoors."
— *Alice Walker*

Soon after the secret elopement, we had a formal wedding in Chicago. I couldn't deprive my parents of seeing me get married. It was a lovely quaint service at my sister's penthouse overlooking Lake Shore Drive. My parents found a Rabbi who looked like an actor from central casting. He wore Bermuda shorts, and he said he was going boating after the service. He also announced that he was leaving his position as a Rabbi, and then made a pass at me behind closed doors. I don't know where my parents found this character, but they did the best they could since our regular Rabbi had passed away.

Upon returning from Chicago, we moved to Newport Beach and there was a little Gelson's in the heart of town. I visited daily to buy groceries for dinner; playing house was new and exciting.

We lived at Promontory Point, an apartment complex overlooking Balboa Island and the Pacific Ocean. This was John

Wayne's territory. Mimicking Ryan O'Neil and Ali McGraw as newlyweds, we rode our bikes on sunny beautiful beach days.

The island had an authentic Chinese restaurant with superb dim sum and fried egg rolls. This two-block area was charming with little mom 'n' pop shops and especially the Balboa Bar ice cream stand. On hot summer nights, the highlight of the evening was their smooth ice cream bar dipped first in chocolate and then in chopped pecans. This concoction still makes my mouth drool just thinking about it. Overall, it felt like a New England town, and we dined there regularly. Life was good.

One year later, my husband joined Sonnebleck/Goldman, a limited partnership firm that required us to move back to Los Angeles. It was a golden opportunity. We found a charming apartment in Marina del Rey Beach. I was teaching part-time and often traveled with my husband on his job assignments with all expenses paid. At home, we entertained on weekends with guacamole, dips and chips, veggies, and bakery goods. My husband's parents or our friends would swing by and snack at the pool or beach.

After a couple of years, the traveling with his job became a grind for David; we were glad when he was offered a great position with a law firm in Newport Beach. Once again, we moved back to the beach and I returned to my first Gelson's. They say there is nothing like your first love, and this marked the beginning of my Gelson's love affair.

In 1980, we settled in a new house in Irvine, ten minutes from Gelson's. Our neighborhood, Turtle Rock, was very quiet with new housing everywhere. I greeted the cows on our hillside and missed the exciting city life.

Walking around the block to beat the boredom only made me feel more isolated. New dusty construction and sparse areas of land made this an underdeveloped neighborhood. Early morning walks made it seem like a scene from *The Twilight Zone.* I didn't yet have a social network there, so I decided to get another degree in Special Education at UC Irvine.

In November 1981, we took a weekend trip to Las Vegas. We were having a marvelous time laughing and eating, and the energy of the city gave us a boost. We stayed at the MGM Hotel where we got married, and it was still the most luxurious hotel in the desert. The dice were thrown, cards were being dealt, and the slot machines were ringing.

On the casino floor, David enjoyed gambling and I played a little blackjack without winning. I remember that we ate corned beef sandwiches and soup at the Deli, one of the hotel's five restaurants. We went to bed quite late, only to hear commotion in the hallway. This didn't seem unusual at first; this was Vegas and there are no rules. We thought perhaps it was just a bunch of late-night partiers.

As the noise continued, David reached for the phone to call the front desk, but the phone was dead. He then went to the window and looked out to discover the hotel was on fire. The billows of smoke were so thick that we could not see the other parts of the building. David shouted, "This place is on fire and we have to get out of here!"

I froze, not knowing what to do. David quickly threw on his clothes and started to dress me, sensing that I was paralyzed with fear. I remember him helping me get into my cowboy boots. As we ran down the hall, we saw people panicking. Smoke was quickly filling the halls as people were yelling and screaming. Suddenly, we found ourselves with nowhere to go.

Thankfully, we didn't try to take the elevator; ten people perished trying to escape that way. I told David that we should take the stairwell, but he did not agree and that saved our lives. A pile of bodies was found one level below our 17th floor, because all the doors were locked, and people could not escape. Smoke inhalation took their lives.

Suddenly, we found a room door slightly open, and we noticed a small balcony adjoining the suite. Two men in the suite invited us to join them. I went around the bar and snagged a bottle of liquor to numb myself. I have no idea what it was because I rarely drink any alcohol other than wine.

Joining us on the narrow balcony were two doctors attending a conference at the hotel and an elderly woman. The men were crying, and the woman was frantic. My husband persuaded her not to jump as she threw her purse over the rail. He saved her life as he did mine.

We viewed people from across the way break windows and tie sheets to escape. One person did jump, and many died on our floor. We feared for our lives, seeing no way out. From head to toe, I was blackened by the smoke. But after two hours of saying goodbye to each other and waiting for our demise, two firefighters in gas masks surprised us by sliding the doors open.

They had two extra masks for us, with a plan to carry the women down first. As we entered the stairwell, one of the firemen swooped me up and carried me down seventeen flights of stairs. Wow! To this day, I greet all firefighters with great gratitude and tell them my story. Sometimes I bake cookies for our local firefighters to thank them for their service.

I was taken to Sunrise Hospital by ambulance as I heard screaming chaos and hovering helicopters. Soon, David and I were reunited after he entered the emergency room. For some reason, our ankles were mistakenly tagged DOA - dead on arrival.

We were permitted to share a room and we remained there for a couple of days. We were visited by a priest who knew about the grim discoveries. That is when we learned about the pile of bodies, one floor below ours, trapped in the stairwell and the elevator tragedy.

Both of us were in shock. As we returned to the hotel to retrieve our things, my mother saw me standing in line in front of the hotel on *CNN*. It almost killed her to view this horrific tragedy and to realize that David and I could both be dead.

We walked up the stairwell with the ghosts of the less fortunate souls to get our possessions. We were one of the first people to pass the blackened rooms viewing luggage, money on dressers, and a disarray of belongings. As dazed and confused as we were, we quickly got our things and hurried out of the building. Returning to the scene became a permanent memory for months, causing many sleepless nights.

We later found out that at 5:00 am, a giant fireball had burst through the Deli's doors, destroying the casino and spreading smoke vertically to the guestroom floors. Within fifteen minutes the event had claimed eighty-seven lives, mostly by smoke inhalation. Over 650 people were injured in the 26-story building.

This fire was the worst disaster in Nevada history and the third worst hotel fire in modern US history, after the 1946 Winecoff Hotel fire in Atlanta that killed 119 people and The San Juan Dupont Plaza Hotel fire on December 31, 1986, in which ninety-seven perished.

The MGM Grand had no alarms or fire sprinklers. In the aftermath, building codes in Nevada were ungraded to require any building open to the public to have fire sprinklers, smoke detectors in rooms and elevators, and exit maps.

When we returned home, we were both experiencing post-traumatic stress. David had a hard time driving on freeways and crossing bridges. I was fearful of indoor parking lots and elevators. To this day, I won't stay above the fifth floor in hotel rooms, and I still do not like elevators. We saw a therapist for a couple of months.

After six months, David returned to normal, but it was the beginning of panic attacks for me. There have been many California fires lately, and that makes me very nervous. I will fly on a plane without too much discomfort, but I won't go on a boat.

This is from a girl who has traveled alone and moved solo to California hardly knowing a soul. I have retaken control from panic attacks through meditation, therapy, and yoga. That awful experience and its effect on me has made me more compassionate toward others who suffer.

If there can be a silver lining to such a tragic event, I wrote a screenplay about the fire, appropriately named *Panic*. It was optioned as a movie-of-the week by Stephen J. Cannell Productions and Gross-Weston Productions. There is also a published book: *The Day the MGM Grand Hotel Burned* by Deirdre Coakley with graphic pictures of this horrific fire.

Just a few weeks after the fire, I found out I was pregnant after trying to conceive for two years. Sadly, I miscarried after ten weeks, perhaps due to the stress of the fire. Some depression understandably followed. Too often, we don't talk openly about loss or process it the right way. This loss, and the loss of control I felt from the fire, were brewing in my psyche and would manifest in future anxiety.

We had been through a series of fertility tests before the fire, and I can clearly remember that day when we found out why we were having a hard time getting pregnant. I nervously drove to that doctor's office to meet David and find out the results. I prepared for what I would say in case David was the infertile one. Enroute, I rehearsed my speech: "Sweetie, I love you and we can adopt a baby."

The doctor informed us that David's sperm was so potent that he would qualify as a sperm donor. Upon exiting the clinic, David practically kicked the door open with his cowboy boot, so proud of his results. That left me as the infertile one. My progesterone was too low at the time of conception.

Six months after the miscarriage, we again decided to try to have a baby. Our new infertility specialist, Dr. S., had auburn hair and a calm bedside manner. He told us that he would get us pregnant again. He gave me a shot of hCG (a hormone therapy) and started me on the fertility drug Clomid.

Now with Dr. S.'s guidance and medical science, I became pregnant after four years of marriage. We were seated at our kitchen table when I told David the good news. I handed him a gift box to surprise him. I anxiously watched him unravel the tissue paper inside the box that contained only a blue plastic diaper.

He was stunned, with his jaw agape as he processed the news. It was the same slightly overwhelmed look he had when we were getting married in Las Vegas; when we were choosing our gold wedding bands, the owner of the jewelry store had to get a chair and a glass of water for him as the reality sunk in. He now had the same chalky look when I told him about the baby. He was already sitting down, so I only had to fetch the glass of water.

I think that many men experience a similarly ambivalent feeling about such a looming lifelong responsibility. Still, we both were thrilled, and David's excitement grew with each month. He needed those nine months to absorb the reality. It's a big leap for some to know that they will never again have freedom as they've known it.

My brother at age 40 said that having two babies eighteen months apart is heaven and hell. That is very telling for all of us. I often hear women say, "I just loved being pregnant." Me? I threw up every day the first time, but I loved raising my babies. Let's face it, it's not always a picnic.

I was fully engaged in creating the nursery. Being a teacher, I bought twenty-six A-to-Z wood letters from the hardware store. We painted them in primary colors and David enthusiastically hung the letters on the wall. Primary colors were known to stimulate the baby's brain, and we wanted to nurture our newborn's intelligence. The yellow walls were complemented with a chunky white crib and (of course) primary-colored balloons. White eyelet curtains adjoined the white shutters, and the finished room could have been featured in a home décor magazine.

Rarely anticipating the sleepless nights to follow, prospective parents often idealize the preparation for the birth of our babies. Yes, it's thrilling, but be prepared for the transition that no one tells you about. The initial adjustment is so challenging. We didn't have a chance to take baby classes due to an early delivery. It took us forty-five minutes to figure out how to diaper a baby. David also had to fetch the masking tape to secure the diaper.

My Gelson's jaunts saved me during this time right before and after the birth of baby Lauren. We often chose to stay closer to home because it was easier with a newborn. Today, there is a new Gelson's in Irvine as well as in the Marina del Rey neighborhood, but I missed out on both stores. We had one generic grocery store and one Bob's Big Boy restaurant. Whoop! My husband was home every night. We were a party of three listening to Neil Diamond, eating corn and fried chicken, and befriending a few neighbors.

I cooked and baked a lot during that time. My famous sweet and sour meatballs were an appetizer that rocked at gatherings; everyone wanted the recipe. I submitted the recipe to the local Irvine newspaper, and it was selected to be featured in the *Recipe of the Week* column. With one-year-old baby Lauren in my arms and a plate of meatballs on my dining room table, the photographer captured my meatball presentation. I felt productive that week.

Still, I was bored and intellectually starving for Los Angeles. Irvine was very new, isolated, and still rural; cows were grazing in my yard. Packing up the car with the stroller, infant seat, and baby bag felt like a huge production, so my Gelson's trips were limited.

I was lonely, with no social connections or family living close by. I started to experience panic attacks that were related to a thyroid disorder, hormonal changes, unresolved trauma from the fire, and never processing the miscarriage. My husband was also home, and he was not working that first year. We had a mortgage, a new baby, a nervous mother, and no obvious way to navigate the situation. Life was difficult.

FIREMEN CHOCOLATE CHIP COOKIES

INGREDIENTS
- 2 1/2 cups all-purpose flour
- 1 tsp kosher salt
- 3/4 tsp baking soda
- 1/2 tsp baking powder
- 3/4 cup room temperature unsalted butter
- 1 cup light brown sugar
- 1/2 cup white sugar
- 2 large eggs
- 1 1/2 tsp pure vanilla extract
- 8 ounces dark chocolate cut into chunks
- 8 ounces semisweet chocolate chips

DIRECTIONS
- Preheat oven to 350 degrees F
- Line two baking sheets
- Mix dry ingredients together
- Beat the soft butter and sugars in the bowl
- Add the eggs, one at a time; beat in the vanilla
- Add the flour mixture and beat until combined
- Fold chocolate into the mixture; form into small balls and flatten
- Bake for 15 minutes or until golden brown; let cool and enjoy
- Serve with Jasmine tea

CHAPTER 5

BEL AIR

"While her lips talk culture, her heart was planning
to invite him to tea."

— *E. M. Forster*

A Fairy Godmother must have sprinkled some magic dust on us. My husband developed a personal finance TV show, *Financial Inquiry*. I helped him with scheduling the guests and I found a furniture store that donated a full set of furniture in return for advertising their store in the credits at the end of the show.

We were returning to Los Angeles, and I was delighted. I would be with city people again among a plethora of interesting restaurants. I would also be back with my friends and family. Despite the cute suburban house that we had, Irvine lacked the verve of city living.

Financial Inquiry became a successful cable TV show overnight. I anchored at the desk to advertise the products sold. It was a mindless job, and the pay was good. My husband was the moderator, and as host he spoke easily and naturally on the subject matter. His guests included famous politicians, stock brokerage CEOs, gold and silver dealers, and other people well-known to the financial world.

During the same time, David also produced many infomercials for celebrities, and he loved it. As an educator, I had little knowledge or interest in the financial world. When we were being interviewed on a different TV show, the host asked me what I thought about "free enterprise." I had no idea what she was talking about. At another local station, the program director asked me to try out for an anchor position and I foolishly replied that I was a teacher, not a TV personality. Back then, I lacked confidence; today I would jump at the chance.

Before we were married, David had acted as an extra on TV and movie sets while in law school. He became a hand model; his were the hands that lit the match in the opening credits of the series *Mission Impossible.* Pretty impressive, huh? Flipping channels at two in the morning, we would see his hands light the match. He had bit parts in many series and appeared in a national beer commercial that paid for law school.

He never strove to be a serious actor, but parts often came his way. He was the next-door neighbor playing a fireman on the sit-com *He and She* with Richard Benjamin and Paula Prentess. Serving as an extra in *Camelot* with Richard Burton and Vanessa Redgrave was one of the most exciting jobs, and the gig lasted six months.

Because of his TV show, we moved to the outer part of Bel Air with its abundance of mansions and movie stars. As I fixed up a modest four-bedroom townhouse just off Mulholland and Beverly Glen, I became friendly with my neighbors. I went to the local park with my now 18-month-old daughter Lauren, and I was expecting my second child, Ashlie.

We frequently entertained on the weekend, and we would mingle with other parents. I loved the *Mommy and Me* classes at the

Stephen S. Wise Temple, and we met a lot of families. The panic attacks subsided, and life seemed manageable. I did have a few mild attacks after Ashlie was born, but I think the post-partum shift in hormones was the cause.

One day, when driving home on Mulholland after a Mommy and Me class, I did have a full-blown panic attack in which I flagged down a police car and asked him to follow me home. He was very kind and honored my request. I'm lucky he didn't make me walk a sober line because I was totally unglued.

I think of the many years when I did not receive the proper therapy for this ailment. Today, anxiety disorders are better diagnosed and understood, and there are treatment options. A combination of yoga, meditation, medication, Buddhist philosophy, and cognitive therapy proved to be my winning ticket.

I am genuinely appreciative that this struggle has been part of my life. It has shaped who I am today, a person with a little extra compassion for others. It's all part of the journey. Someone once told me that experiencing the wide array of emotions with life's up and downs only adds to your character, like a bottle of fine red wine.

Life returned to normal for us, and my anxiety subsided as we became a typical suburban family. Grocery shopping and entertaining drew my interest into the culinary arts; cookbooks and cooking classes were a major passion. I fully enjoyed being a mom, a wife, a homemaker, a chef, a decorator. I embraced the role of making our house a real home. Unlike my childhood, there was a lot of love and laughter to accompany the good wholesome meals. This was, for us in the 1980s, a Norman Rockwell moment in time.

There was a Gelson's at the Century City shopping center and one just off Ventura. We lived smack in the middle at the top of the canyon and pretty far from Gelson's, but it was always well worth the drive. A typical weekend might include barbecues and potluck dinners. Someone might bring a Campbell's soup con-coction, but most guests would bring great dips, appetizers, and desserts. I started to invest in high end cookbooks, and we felt that this settled life was especially good.

David's hard work paid off as his successful television show expanded to a national audience, with a parade of distinguished financial and political guests. After a long week, we would go out to dinner on Friday night. We fell in love with this little new restaurant off Sunset Boulevard called Spago's. Of course, we had no inkling that it would become one of the world's most famous restaurants. Today, Wolfgang Puck is a legend and I've even bought his pots and pans on the Home Shopping Network.

David befriended Wolfgang and became one of his investors in the Prescott Hotel and the Postrio restaurant in San Francis-co. Often, we dined there and stayed in that quaint boutique hotel featuring French decor and antiques. The bathrooms were designed with spa-inspired luxury touches; it was inviting and visually relaxing with white fluffy bath robes and towels. Down-stairs from the hotel guest quarters, the restaurant was one of the first with an open kitchen where the guests would be entertained watching the chefs perform their magic.

The investors were invited every New Year's Eve and we were housed on a private floor. Just outside our hotel room door, the champagne overflowed as the guests snacked on Wolfgang's signature pizza creations. Later in the evening, we would dine at this five-star restaurant. This was our yearly vacation, and we often brought the girls. It was one of the happiest times.

ENTERTAINING FOR A CROWD - CHICKEN MARBELLA

INGREDIENTS
- 1/4 cup olive oil
- 1/4 cup red wine vinegar
- 1 cup pitted prunes
- 1/2 cup pitted green olives
- 1/2 cup capers
- 6 bay leaves
- 8 cloves of garlic, peeled and minced
- 2 tsp salt
- 1/4 tsp ground pepper
- 1 tsp of Beau Monde seasoning
- 2 cut-up chickens, 3-4 pounds each
- 1 cup white wine
- 1 cup brown sugar
- 2 tbsp chopped flat-leaf parsley

DIRECTIONS
- Preheat oven to 350 degrees F
- In a large bowl, combine chicken, oil, vinegar, bay leaves, garlic, salt, pepper
- Marinate overnight if possible, or 3-4 hours
- Add the wine, brown sugar, olives, capers, and prunes
- Arrange on baking sheet and baste every 15 minutes
- Bake for 50-60 minutes
- Sprinkle with parsley and serve

CHAPTER 6

MOM

"You can never get a cup of tea large enough
or a book long enough to suit me."
— *C.S. Lewis*

My mother was a magnificent cook who never used a recipe. Best known for her exquisite duck, she would multitask in the kitchen making spaghetti and meatballs, a roast, and possibly some buttered shrimp. She was like a short-order cook who had something delicious for everyone. I never saw my mother sit down and eat with us; working off her nervous energy, she would taste and serve and then taste and serve again.

Mom moved to California in 1986, and entertaining the grand-parents with our two toddlers became the norm. Food remained a key focal point; we had a celebration for every holiday and the meal preparation sometimes took days. We were fortunate to have a nurturing housekeeper, Moray, who the girls adored. She was a skillful cook, and we loved her specialties like vegetable egg rolls or fish and rice. The girls especially enjoyed the picnics with Moray, who was a part of our family for five years. We all loved her.

My mom had two Gelson's stores near her house, one in Encino and one in Reseda. I would take her shopping and sit at the coffee bar drinking iced tea. After a while, I would find her gabbing away with the staff. Of course, they knew everything about me and my family. But that is what made mom so special; people gravitated to her warmth. She always addressed the employees by their names.

After Gelson's, we would go to her condo and eat all the groceries. She would serve everything that she bought and then some, including sushi, deli meats, cherries, and cookies from the bakery. Even if you weren't hungry, she still prepared the smorgasbord. Mom loved to feed people.

I would carry the iced tea with me, and the caffeine buzz always fueled my brain throughout the day. Typically, I took Mom shopping at Gelson's twice a week to get my caffeine fix and to visit with her. Mom was my rock and my mentor. With her soft-spoken voice, she always had the right answers to any issue, and she taught me to be a lady. Whenever I had a problem, her words spoke to me. When I shared a dilemma, she would often say with her calm demeanor, "What is, is." Today, some psychologists and self-help authors are making a lot of money with their books dedicated to this same concept.

My mother had a great sense of humor, and we would have laughing fits over the silliest things. One day at a Chinese restaurant, our booth faced another booth where we noticed a woman who was my mother's doppelgänger. She had the same short blonde hairstyle, but we saw only the back of her head. My mom noticed thinning hair on the top of this woman's head and said, "That looks just like me, bald spot and all."

We were hysterical, and we couldn't even speak when the server came to take our order. We had tears rolling down our cheeks. We finally had to ask to be moved to another table because we could not stop looking at this woman's bald spot and we could not pull ourselves together.

My husband's mother was a lovely woman. It was a sad day when she passed. Like my father, she had suffered for years with Alzheimer's disease. My mother and I were attending the funeral along with the family, but just before the graveside service, Mom had to use the bathroom. After what seemed like a long delay, the others were waiting for us. I became concerned and went to check on her in the bathroom.

Another woman in the bathroom asked me immediately if my mom's name was Janet. As I answered yes, my mom reported out from the bathroom stall that she couldn't get her pantyhose up. I saw her ankles below the stall door with her pantyhose tightly wrapped around her ankles. I couldn't stop laughing; eventually, she managed to pull them up or off.

Finally, at the grave site, I resumed laughing when I couldn't get that image out of my mind; I quickly put my hands over my face. By that point, my body was vibrating from laughter; people were patting me on the back to comfort me, thinking I was crying.

My mom was an attractive widow during the 1990s, and the older men at Gelson's would often approach to ask for her help picking out a good tomato. But after spending three intense years caring for my father before he died of Alzheimer's, mom said she has no intention of taking care of another aging man.

One day we viewed an elderly white-haired woman who was stooped over her shopping cart and shuffling her feet at Gelson's. As we watched her, she suddenly stopped and passed gas, and then continued to shuffle on. Stopped again, did it again, and then shuffled on. We both watched this three-step dance: shuffle, stop, fart. Shuffle, stop, fart. My mom was amused, but also appalled. Her eyes rolled and she said, "Get me out of here."

We left promptly, only to find ourselves at a local deli where we saw more senior citizens eating corn beef sandwiches and matzo ball soup. Mom didn't enjoy being around old people. Yet she assisted the elderly people in her building and had great compassion for all people who suffered for any reason.

She would invite her building's janitor to lunch, serving a delicious home-cooked meal on her good China, with a cloth napkin and ginger ale in a wine glass. Later she would buy some gifts for his small children. Mom had a heart as big as Texas but was never comfortable around older folks. She didn't mind the thought of aging or even dying (although she said she would miss eating buttered sweet corn). That was Mom.

When I was fifteen years old, I read a Harold Robbins' book about a woman engaging in oral sex with a man. I wasn't aware of this form of lovemaking. Remember, I grew up in the sixties and in the Midwest. Women were still virgins when they got married; some of them, anyway. I brought the book to my mother to read this passage and give me her take on it. I was shocked. When I asked her if women really performed this act, she responded, "Oh yes they do, but Jewish girls don't do that."

She also told me women have sex with their husbands only to please them. Mom was somewhat cold in that regard, rarely showing affection toward my father. She didn't like to be hugged. I'm sure this had to do with her early years, having been raised in an orphanage.

Before she moved to California, she would visit us in Bel Air. My generous husband took all of us to Adriano's, a swanky and sophisticated Italian Restaurant in The Glen where the waiters were probably making a six-figure salary. In Bel Air, many celebrities were often seen at these fancy restaurants. It wasn't unusual to spot Clint Eastwood, Johnny Carson, or Jaclyn Smith dining in this artisan decor restaurant.

My mom loved Adriano's, and the suave Italian waiter was paying a lot of attention to her. She was beautiful, smartly dressed and sporting a champagne mink stole. Then she asked him if he had ever tried the clam chowder at Denny's. He smiled and replied, "No, Signora, I have not" and then he winked at me.

My sister and I were hysterically laughing. Although Mom looked like a queen, she had revealed that she was one of the common folks at heart. That was Mom – an unpretentious woman with her own style. David and I were regulars at Adriano's, and we loved this waiter; we saw him almost every Friday night.

My mother had a twin sister and three other siblings; they all lost their mother to the 1918 flu epidemic when Mom was eighteen months old. Her father Jacob Smith was a decent man who could not handle the load of five motherless children. The Smith children were welcomed into the Marks Nathan orphanage home in Chicago in 1918.

The orphanage was founded with a $15,000 contribution from the estate of Marks Nathan, a turn of the century businessman who believed the community needed an orphanage that practiced the principles of Orthodox Judaism. Typically, Jewish orphans were consigned to the streets or passed around from relative to relative in the crowded tenement neighborhood.

Orphanage director Elias Trotsky believed in the power of culture and discipline with a lot of love, joy, and laughter. This was the Jewish tradition and many wealthy European immigrants contributed funds to support this much needed home. Every child was given a Hebrew education and music lessons. Shabbat dinners were served every Friday night just prior to the religious services.

My mom said the food was often very good and wholesome, made with old-country recipes from the Russian Jews. In my experience, the Jewish and Italian peoples share a love for cooking, although the deliciously fattening meals can be the reason for future heart bypass surgery.

Children at the orphanage made frequent visits to symphony concerts and stage plays, with tickets provided by members of the board of trustees. Mom learned tap dancing, enjoyed summer camp, and had a love for reading because of the in-home library. The children were required to spend an hour reading after school before they could go out and play. Although motherless, mom had many role models there; she keenly remembered one administrator who favored her. Occasionally, a very kind teacher would take my mom to a downtown cultural event.

Although many people perceived orphanages as a Victorian-era nightmare, this home was different. Many of the children grew up to be doctors, lawyers, and astute business leaders.

The 100-year anniversary of the home was celebrated in 1992 with a reunion in Chicago. Many accomplished and successful people from all over the country attended, including my mother who reunited with her twin and old friends. The home had produced such luminaries as a constitutional law expert, a baseball Hall of Fame member, a Chicago Tribune sportswriter, and Barney Ross, world welterweight boxing champion. Before every fight as an adult, he would go back and visit with the kids at the home.

From 1906 until the close of World War II, this orphanage was a place of refuge for Jewish children who were struggling with the lack of love, support, education, and structure. Most of the three hundred beds were occupied by boys and girls who had lost parents to diseases or accidents. This marvelous facility saved many lives. Perhaps we would have fewer criminals and drug abusers if we offered the homeless the same kindness and facilities.

The Marks Nathan Home was closed in 1947 due to changing social policy; this type of large-scale institution was no longer supported. Still, this particular home should be a model to house our homeless children nationally.

In California, The Orange County Children's Home is well-known, successful, and has thousands of local supporters. A couple of times a year I have offered a workshop there, *The Authentic Self Writing Workshop.* It is always a pleasure to see the teens identify their strengths, gifts, and talents through discussions and writing. I'm not sure who gets more out of it, me or the teens. The workshop activities also included the construction of a business-themed collage, and these teens have crafted some beautiful works of art.

The participants developed a stronger sense of purpose by taking on this project. We also talked about self-compassion and living a healthy, holistic lifestyle – mind, body, and spirit. Basic habits like eating healthy were also on the workshop agenda; each teen was charged with developing a meal idea using whole foods.

Compared to an earlier time, people now are more aware about good health and how processed food should be avoided. I walk the perimeter of my Gelson's, eyeing the healthier options among the choices at the deli, meats, dairy, and the produce sections. But every now and then, a fattening dinner is a good splurge for all of us. My mom had two primary meals for our Friday nights dinners – roasted chicken or beef brisket. Here's a typical Shabbat dinner – get your antacid ready!

LALA'S BRISKET

INGREDIENTS
- 5-6 pounds first cut brisket
- 3 tbsp olive oil
- 3 large sweet onions and 3 carrots, cut into ½" pieces
- 2-3 cloves of garlic, minced
- 1 tsp each of paprika, cumin, oregano, salt, and pepper
- 1 tbsp brown sugar
- 2 cups beef broth
- One bottle of Heinz Chili Sauce

DIRECTIONS
- Preheat oven to 350 degrees F
- Put 2 tbsp olive oil in a Dutch oven
- Season brisket with 1 tsp pepper and salt
- Sear all sides in Dutch oven on medium high heat until golden brown
- In large skillet, cook onions in 1 tbsp oil until golden brown
- Stir in garlic and spices
- Stir in 2 cups beef broth and bring to a boil
- Add Heinz Chili Sauce and brown sugar
- Spoon onion mixture over brisket
- Bake covered with lid slightly ajar 3 1/2 hours, basting every hour
- For best results wrap up in tin foil; refrigerate until the next day
- Slice thin and reheat 30 minutes; serve with mashed potatoes or sweet potatoes.

For indigestion, I recommend dandelion tea

CHAPTER 7

CALABASAS

"When she is unable to avoid the matter further,
she makes a pot of tea."

— *Erin Morgenstern*

After Bel Air we moved to Calabasas, which is about twenty miles from Los Angeles. We bought a custom Mediterranean home located behind guarded gates. My husband had wanted to buy his dream home, and rightfully so with the success of his financial television show. This was Calabasas before the Kardashians lived there. The girls could attend the public school, rated number one in the county, and I did not have to schlep all over town.

Moving to the suburbs seemed like the right thing to do, although I had reservations about leaving my nice little Bel Air community. I wasn't accustomed to the heat, and it seemed quite secluded, being surrounded by mountains. Any way you slice it, it was the San Fernando Valley and it was an adjustment for this city girl. I often feel that in California, there are two kinds of people: desert people living in a valley, or water people living at the beach. I love the beach – any beach.

The home was beautiful, greeting you with an open airy feeling the instant you walked through the door. We had three custom-designed fireplaces, and the kitchen was the size of my first apartment. The swimming pool and jacuzzi offered a panoramic view of the whole valley. At night, the lights from the city were glistening. We drank our wine as we gazed at the autumn-colored sunsets. The hues of orange, yellow, and red filled the sky with wonder. The arched doorways and wood floors reflected old-world warmth and charm. The development was called "Vista Pointe" and it was located above a rolling green golf course. How did we land here? Paradise at its best.

Yet, an eerie state of anxiety was brewing in my bones. After moving in, I started to have panic attacks. I missed the old neighborhood and my friends. The suburbs felt weird and isolated to me, especially during the arid hot summers. I had many out-of-body experiences and I tried to stay stable.

The girls were seven and five years old. We went to the local drugstore one afternoon, and as I held both of their hands going up and down the aisles, I felt like we were all little children. I tried to hide my nervousness as the aisles seemed to wobble in and out. I was trying to make this all work; after all, I lived in paradise, right?

It was a new environment and I struggled with the change. David was running his business in Brentwood, an hour away in traffic, and the girls were about to begin classes at a quaint country school in The Hidden Hills community. Horses and estate homes surrounded the school, and this was idyllic country living to a casual observer. I felt like I was in "Green Acres" every time I entered this sprawling community.

Things got better with time as I adapted to my neighborhood. Tending to the house, writing, and planning menus took up most of my time. I was taking some art classes and screenwriting classes at U.C.L.A, which prepared me to author my screenplay about the MGM fire. I followed with a second screenplay, "Papa Rose," which was optioned for Alan King. This seven-year project kept me going while I shuttled the girls to every activity including soccer, Brownies, Hebrew School, and piano lessons.

We lived in Calabasas for ten years. I enjoyed my home, I had nice neighbors, and our family life was thriving. We always had neighborhood children running in and out of our house. During Halloween it looked like a Steven Spielberg movie, with all the kids in their costumes. One might expect ET to be lurking around the corner. Barbecues and swim parties were common on weekends and during the holidays, just as it had been in Bel Air, but I longed to return to life near the water.

We adopted a cat named Sugar and a Yorkshire terrier, Muffy, also known as "The Muff Dog." A rabbit and a frog soon joined the menagerie. It was a healthy environment for my children. We were a very close-knit family with a lot of love, laughter, and living. We were, by most measures, the all-American family.

Food was always our main attraction. One time on a family trip, we all awoke at 3:00 AM in our hotel and we ventured out to find a Carl's Junior so that we could wolf down giant greasy burgers and fries. We laughed so hard that we ended up calling ourselves "The Rollies." That name stuck with us for many years and to this day. We were all goofballs that night aboard the Cuckoo Train.

I sense that many women, as I did, begin to reexamine their lives during their forties. The girls were getting older, and being a mother and wife started to feel less like an adventure and more like a routine. I stopped going to lunch with some of the neighbors because the chit-chat was always so mindless. There was a lack of authentic conversations with some of these women, who cared mostly about decorating, plastic surgery, and gossip. They could have been "The Real Housewives of Calabasas." I continued to miss my interesting and cultured Bel Air friends. I knew that Calabasas was a wholesome neighborhood for our girls, and that is why I stayed for a decade. For a period, my daily life consisted of going through the motions. Something was missing. Did I need to get another degree, cut my hair, or run a marathon?

Finally, it dawned on me that work needed to be done within. It was the beginning of examining my life. When you are a mother with young children, there is no "me." I now felt an itch to explore life through books and the next level of consciousness. This was when I discovered the philosophy of Buddhism before it became the trendy topic on every magazine cover. Thirty years ago, I had a friend from San Diego who helped me on the path. I'm not a Buddhist, but I love the practice and philosophy. It has saved me many times and was the best substitute for Xanax, which I took occasionally.

At times, I felt like I was in an abyss. My middle-aged angst was brewing, and I wanted some answers; only later did I discover that there are no answers. It really was a matter of coming to terms with the enemy — myself.

I had to examine what was clouding my mind. I drove the girls to school and to their after-school classes, but afterwards felt a bit empty inside. This did not feel like a well-lived life. What could possibly be missing? It took a few years and some very good therapy to realize I deserve to be happy. Life does not have all answers, and you cannot rewrite the past. I had entered my journey of self-evaluation.

One must eventually fill the void by becoming the absent part of the mother and the father you never had. There will always be missing pieces, but my journey started with self-compassion. You cannot read this in a book. The "aha" moment is a process of coming to terms with your vulnerability. I had to make peace with the same things that I was taught to hide or be ashamed of. I understood why I yearn for meaningful conversation, focusing on the depth and rainbow of feelings.

I turned to reading books with profound ideas, such as The Tibetan Book of Living and Dying, The Road Less Traveled, Flow, Man's Search for Meaning, The Denial of Death, A Path with Heart, The Drama of the Gifted Child, Living Dharma, Seeking the Heart of Wisdom, and Darkness Visible.

For the first time in my life, I became more introverted. I continued to take writing classes, and I tended to my home and family. Along the way, I did meet insightful people, some in my writing class. The writers I have known are complex humans; we were part of an esoteric group.

It was the right time for me to enter therapy. In hindsight, I can say that it was the optimal solution to explore the abyss with a qualified UCLA therapist. It wasn't that I didn't have a good childhood overall, but there were certainly damaging parts. I was taught to hide all the darkness of childhood and all the secrets.

With therapy, instead of carrying around the "less than" feelings of insecurity, I explored the past by examining the unconscious mindset of the voices from childhood. This is what had given me the feeling of being incomplete. It wasn't a new career or a new pair of shoes that was going to lift my spirits; it was simply learning to live with all the parts. When I did, a sense of peace finally emerged.

It was also time to visit my chapters of disappointment, fear, and sadness: infertility, miscarriages, and PTSD from the MGM fire. Naturally, this took a few years. I can candidly say that my forties and fifties were the best times of feeling personally integrated. It was then, and only then, that I felt good about presenting myself to the outside world. I felt whole. I learned to not only indulge in self-care, but to feel compassion for others. I felt an urge to give back to others. I felt a shift of positive emotions. Joy came back!

When I think back about raising our two accomplished daughters, I have asked myself what would I have done differently? After reviewing many videos of the family events celebrating birthdays, holidays, and simple weekend celebrations, I don't think I would change very much.

As always, food remained front and center. I loved to cook and present a buffet at every major event like Thanksgiving, our favorite holiday. The grandparents brought their goodies and we would eat for hours; second and third helpings were common. The house was filled with the scent of sage and rosemary that lasted well into the evening.

The cool crisp day with orange, yellow, and red floral arrangements throughout the house complemented our table setting. Grandma Eleanor would bring her pecan, lemon, and pumpkin pies while Grandma Janet whipped up her famous green Jell-O mold side dish made with sour cream and mandarin oranges.

Often on weekends, we entertained with some of our old friends from the past. Sizzling barbecue burgers and hot dogs were well tended by chef Daddy David. David's hair caught on fire one Sunday afternoon while he was grilling the meat, and after we extinguished the smoldering flames, the girls were laughing hysterically. We took full advantage of the pool and spa as we all swam, laughed, and screamed with joy.

David bought the girls two giant black and white bear-faced bean bag chairs monogrammed with their names. I remembered when the girls were settled in with their blankets and glued to the TV screen, watching Sesame Street and Punky Brewster, or playing Nintendo and Game Boy.

As an involved dad, David took the girls to amusement parks, shopping malls, movies, and ski trips. Those events created great memories. He also attended every soccer game. He was their hero and still is to this day.

Looking back, I wish I had taken the girls to more educational events over the weekends. Going to museums, libraries, bookstores, and planetariums would have been more stimulating for the girls to build better outside interest. We did these things periodically, but the girls were often bored.

The girls did have many extracurricular activities. When I awoke each morning, I had to focus on what day it was and what events were lined up. I had to remember if the girls had piano lessons, soccer practice, a Brownie meeting, or Hebrew School classes. Who was carpooling and what time do I pick up? How can I be at two places at the same time? Was it Tuesday or Wednesday that I needed to switch the time with my neighbor? When can I sneak in an iced tea and recharge?

I wish I had found a way to volunteer more often with the girls, maybe at a soup kitchen. The girls really needed the experience of being of service to others. We did visit a senior center during the holidays with their Brownie group, but I could have done more.

I recall when we drove by a homeless man near our shopping center the day after Thanksgiving. The girls suggested we go home and make a leftover plate of food for him. Rolling down the window, the girls handed the goodies to this disheveled man. The bearded, dirty, sun-tanned man was grateful and smiled with his missing teeth. I saw delight not only in the man's eyes, but in my children's eyes as well.

The girls did have big hearts and were often thoughtful, such as when they surprised me with breakfast in bed on Mother's Day. An overcooked egg, burnt toast, and love notes were presented on a tray with a flower from our backyard, and homemade gifts followed.

I tried to teach the girls gratitude. On Thanksgiving Day, I would type a personalized note of gratitude and place it on each person's plate at dinner. This started the conversation as others joined in before eating. I told everyone why I was grateful for having them in my life, and it was a lovely moment.

We made plenty of mistakes, but we always made our children the first priority. David had a gentleness with both girls. He tried to tell them about the world; his life lessons, pursuing hard work, and persevering through life. He gave them the power to go after their dreams. David believed in both of his girls, and I think they have carried his voice in their hearts. There was no shortage of joking around, with big helpings of silliness and laughter. From pumpkin cut-outs to dyeing Easter eggs to trick-or treating, he was always the third child. The world was safe with Dad.

We produced fearless daughters with put-away power when it came to food, and they had a fire in their bellies when it came to taking on the world. We did our best with the tools that we had. When our girls became young adults, we were very proud of both. They turned out to be responsible, productive, successful, educated, young women. What more could we ask for?

Our time in Calabasas yielded memorable days, except for one year. I struggled with a debilitating illness right after the death of my father. I had always had good health, and even to this day my blood scores are excellent. But I was under a lot of stress.

We owned two houses, but when we tried to sell, market conditions made it impossible. I was exhausted by the combination of that housing stress, frequent trips visiting my father in the hospital, and the obligations of raising our children. I came down with a flu and fever that never went away.

My husband and mother thought I was going to die. I couldn't eat much, and I was wasting away. My energy was gone; I could hardly walk to the bathroom. My speech was slurred, and I had impairment with my short-term memory. I finally saw a neurologist at UCLA, and he diagnosed this mysterious illness as a form of encephalitis.

I slowly improved, but it took eighteen months. I know some people never recover. Experts better understand these viruses today than during my struggle. It is not a psychiatric illness, but stress is surely a factor. I am thankful every day for my full recovery and continued good health.

After ten memorable years, it was time to leave Calabasas. Gelson's had built a state-of-the-art grocery store nearby during our last year there. It was huge, with not one but two coffee bar areas where one could get food and beverage. When it opened, I went there to write, re-charge, buy groceries, or meet a friend for an iced tea. We didn't get the full experience of this spectacular Gelson's because we soon moved back to Newport Beach for the third and last time. We both had new business opportunities open to us, and the aqua blue water was calling our names.

Calabasas was a great place to raise children and our girls have many fond childhood memories that can never be replaced. It was the core of family living with a full mix of drama and a lot of love. Child rearing had its share of challenges, especially during their teenage years. On the difficult days, I would always say, "When all else fails, make fudge."

FABULOUS FUDGE

INGREDIENTS
- 3 cups of Guittard semi-sweet chocolate chips
- 1 14 oz. can sweetened condensed milk
- Dash of salt
- 1 cup of pecans or walnuts
- 1 tsp vanilla extract

DIRECTIONS
- In a saucepan, melt chips over low heat and add milk and salt
- Remove from heat and stir in nuts and vanilla
- Spread evenly into a wax paper lined 8-inch square pan
- Chill 2 hours or until firm
- Turn fudge over onto cutting board, peel off waxed paper and cut into squares
- Enjoy with oolong tea

Chapter 8

1998: BACK TO NEWPORT BEACH

"When I drink tea, I am conscious of peace.
The core breath of heaven rises in my sleeves,
and blows my cares away."

— *Lo Tung*

We returned to Newport Beach in 1998, leaving the San Fernando Valley because we were weary of the heat, and we wanted to return to the water. It was a wonderful community to raise the girls, but David and I are not valley people; we were both brought up near the water.

I immediately landed a job with the school district as a special education teacher. At my interview, I wore a simple black dress, a strand of pearls, and low black heels (bonus, I was having a good hair day). I had confidence going in, but I hadn't worked as an educator since I was in my twenties.

This was my only interview, and it went very well. The administrator, who was also the head of special education, quickly ordered the paperwork for me to sign. She was a lovely lady, and we were chatting like old friends for an hour, sharing stories about our families, and defining our philosophy regarding education, children, and learning disabilities. We conversed easily during the interview and found that we had many things in common.

Despite my confidence going in, I was in shock to suddenly transition to an officially employed 47-year-old woman. I had to splash water on my face in the bathroom because I started to panic. I arrived thinking this was just an interview; I didn't anticipate that she would put a contract under my nose to sign.

I had known that the district was running out of time to fill the position. I was certified with three credentials in special education, and I had superior ratings from my work in two previous school districts. I didn't have a prison record and I looked pretty normal.

But I saw my open schedule coming to an end. Yikes! It was time to run to Gelson's and stew this over with an iced tea and a cheese Danish. Could I really commit to a full-time job? What about going out to lunch or just hanging out? Big decision! This reminded me of Goldie Hawn in the movie *Private Benjamin* when she enlisted in the army with her *Louis Vuitton* bag.

I soon discovered that this new job was the best thing that could have happened to me. My children were teen-agers, I was new to the area, and I was well qualified with my experience, academic background, and credentials. I had been out of the workforce for so long, it was like being thrown into water to sink or swim.

However, I quickly regained proficiency in creating programs for the students' needs and testing for learning disabilities while working with the school psychologist. I developed an individual educational program for each child according to their academic level and style of learning. I realized that this was my niche.

I was part administrator and part teacher with a learning lab that offered resources for these students. I had the various special education groups coming and going hourly from their home room classes with a full-time aide. To match their style of learning, the students needed the kind of individual programs that could not be provided in the general classroom, especially for students with reading disabilities. The paperwork was extensive, and the meetings were either in the early morning hours or late after school hours. I was the therapist, nurse, teacher, and problem solver to all.

When I had first graders to test, I took the time to make each child comfortable before testing. I would sit on the floor with them in the reading corner and offer a cookie because that always broke up the formality.

I remember when little Johnny asked, "When is your mommy picking you up?" He thought I was a peer, not a teacher. It was obvious he wanted to go home. But after the morning testing and lots of interaction, he didn't want to leave. He was so adorable that I wanted to take him home. That is how my endorphins were elevated and how much I really did love my career.

I always left the house twenty minutes early for a stop at Gelson's to pick up an iced tea. The caffeine jumpstarts my brain for the day, but I still loved to return for a refill after work. Some people relax by going to bars after a day's work, but I would go to Gelson's coffee bar. I always order a large iced tea, no fruit, no ice, no sugar. This was my simple pleasure after a long day of work.

I grew to love my job as I did when I taught in Chicago and Los Angeles. I didn't have to dig deep to find my passion for teaching. The interaction with special education students is so fulfilling. I met many scared or troubled children, and it was my job to first build up their self-esteem and then discover their learning style. All students can succeed. There are no disabled students, only disabled teaching methods. That was my motto.

My personal relationship with each student over the years gave me a rich and fulfilling life. A bulletin board with notes, dates, and memos hung above my desk; in the center I posted a quote that inspired me to do my best every day.

"One hundred years from now it will not matter what kind of car I drove, what kind of house I lived in, how much money I had, nor what my clothes looked like. But the world may be a little better, the universe a little brighter, because I was important to a child."
– Author Unknown

On any given day, I savored my daily ritual of drinking iced tea at Gelson's before running off to the demands of the moment. Folks at the coffee bar would be chatting with each other, buzzing about current events. Like the TV series *Cheers,* it truly was a place where everybody knows your name.

Although I have been to almost all the other Gelson's, I call the one in Newport Beach my home. It is one of the oldest, and it's not very big or fancy. Prior to returning to Newport Coast, I flirted with other Gelson's including Calabasas, Encino, Reseda, Century City, Pacific Palisades, and more. Still, nothing compares to the quaint and cozy Gelson's in Newport Beach.

The Newport Beach Gelson's has added a tapas bar in the coffee bar. Along with tea or coffee, you can now get a glass of wine, an appetizer, or one of Wolfgang's pizzas. I'm particularly fond of their bagel sandwich with lox, onions, capers, and tomato. You can go for breakfast and have an egg sandwich, or oatmeal with blueberries, banana, and nuts. Why go anywhere else?

The employees all know me and my family, and when I enter the coffee bar, they prepare my iced tea as soon as our eyes meet. Happy conversation follows, as well as greetings from the other mellow customers. The coffee clerks are an amazing, hard-working, friendly bunch. They know almost everyone on a first name basis, and they get your order even before you say a word.

As noted in the first chapter, Bernie was one of the cast of characters that defined the vibe at Gelson's coffee bar. Like me, this nonagenarian gentleman hailed from Chicago but had lived in Southern California most of his adult life. Bernie was a widower, and all the women made a fuss over him. I was no exception. Bernie with his newspaper, bagel, and hot tea always had a happy smile for everyone sitting at the same table.

Bernie was my *Tuesdays with Morrie* friend. I loved his wisdom and his personal journey in life. Many times, we drove to Gelson's together when Bernie's car was on the brink. One day when I had made chicken soup, I discovered that Bernie was not feeling well. I brought Bernie and his daughter to my home and I served them the soup. He was so appreciative, and it was a nice way to spend the afternoon. Of course, the soup was made with Gelson's fresh chicken.

Gelson's also carries a delicious rôtisserie chicken. Whenever I had leftovers from that plump rosemary-garlic chicken, I would use it to make an incredible chicken soup. You can't beat the freshness or purity of their chickens. This soup is perfect anytime, but particularly so if you are under the weather with a cold. It's Gelson's penicillin.

Bernie passed at age ninety-six, and it was a very sad day. Flowers adorned his table at Gelson's for the week. He went out on top with a positive attitude and a life well-lived.

CHICKEN SOUP

INGREDIENTS
- 1 whole chicken
- 64 ounces (two boxes or 4.5 cans) of nonfat organic chicken broth or homemade bone broth
- 3 tbsp olive oil
- 1 onion
- 6 carrots
- 1 turnip
- 3 celery sticks
- 1 tbsp each thyme and fresh dill
- Optional - 1 tsp Beau Monde seasoning (salt seasoned with celery and onion)

DIRECTIONS
- Shred chicken. Discard skin and gristle. Save the bones, set aside the meat
- Slice vegetables into chunks
- In a large pot, sauté onion, carrots, turnip, and celery in the olive oil
- Add broth and chicken bones, cook on a low heat for 40 minutes until veggies are tender
- Add thyme and fresh dill
- Add Beau Monde seasoning
- Add the chicken for 20 minutes and simmer; don't overcook
- Boil (separate pot) one 10 oz package of refrigerated tortellini or 8 oz of egg noodles
- Add tortellini or noodles to the soup; enjoy!

At Gelson's I befriended Patty, a second-grade teacher who visited the coffee bar with her son Michael. Patty and I had a lot in common. We were the same age, we were baby boomers, we were teachers, and we treasured our ritual at Gelson's.

I decided to play Cupid and fix up Patty with my husband's best friend, Jerry. Jerry was divorced and looking for companionship. We made plans and soon we were entertaining Patty and Jerry in my home as we feasted on appetizers and take-out Chinese food. With a little wine and a little soft jazz music, it began to look like a scene from *Sex and The City,* middle-aged style. Romance was in the air.

Sparks flew, and the new couple left our home to have a drink at a local restaurant. Their courtship had an easy pace, and then two and a half years later, my husband and I traveled to the Santa Ana Courthouse to witness the union of Patty and Jerry. The four of us posed for a picture in front of Gelson's right after the wedding. I shared that photo with the market, and it soon appeared in the Gelson's newsletter.

Although I claim some responsibility for fixing up these two lovebirds, I also credit Gelson's. Perhaps if Patty and Jerry were to expand their families, the newborn might be named Gelson. No further children are in their current plans, but it isn't unlikely or unreasonable to someday tell Gelson to fetch a bone.

DATE NIGHT MENU

On a mirrored or bamboo tray, sort the following finger foods in groups. Add some parsley sprigs throughout the platter.

- Charcuterie platter
- Variety of cheeses like St. Agur blue cheese, rosemary goat cheese, brie, Beehive brand Ginger-Turmeric Cheddar, or Cranberry-Cinnamon Goat Cheese Log
- Organic grapes
- Marcona almonds
- Variety of olives from the olive bar, including Cerignola
- Petite fresh carrots with the tops
- Breakfast radishes
- Persian cucumber and Anjou sliced pears
- Red, orange, and yellow petite peppers
- Hummus and/or red pepper sauce
- Whole grain crackers and rice crackers (gluten free)

One never needs to dress up while shopping or lounging at Gelson's. I've seen everything from yoga workout clothes to Chanel suits. I would often see new mothers donning baseball caps over long ponytails while schlepping a couple of kiddies in their carts. I see them driving big white SUVs in which they load up the groceries for the week. (Have you ever noticed that all modern cars are white, silver, or black?) On any given day at the coffee bar, local PTA moms are having a meeting, older folks are gathering for socialization, and laptop-toting college students are congregating.

To my dismay, too many plastic surgery nightmares were often visible at Gelson's, and the women in Newport Beach were no exception. The middle-aged women (and sometimes men) would enter the store with faces pulled tight, squinting eyes, and sometimes artificial cheekbones that gave them an alien presence. It reminded me of *The Body Snatchers* or the cast from the movie *Avatar.*

Even the aspiring starlets as young as thirty had oversized lips and improbably voluptuous silicone breasts. I was saddened to witness women approaching seventy with miniskirts, oversized breasts, fake long blonde hair, and an aging mask of plastic surgery. These may be single women looking for a man, but men her age want an actual young woman, not a plastic one. We all could use a little work as we age, but too much is never a good thing. Women are now getting butt implants that resemble the ass of a horse. Is this really progress?

Iris Apfel, born in Queens, is a famous designer and fashion icon who turned one hundred years old in 2021. She's seen enough in her lifetime to remark that plastic surgery can go very wrong and make you look like a Picasso painting, yet so many persist in the surgical pursuit of the fountain of youth. The power of their egos astounds me, but I appreciate that it's hard to grow old and lose your looks.

We'd all do better by having something in our lives that is more important than just the physical appearance of our faces and bodies. There are countless outstanding women who are overweight or "average" looking but their inner personalities, kindness, humor, and accomplishments far exceed those of the plastic Barbie doll surgically-altered crowd. What is the better way to measure one's worth?

But let's return to the diversity of Gelson's shoppers! I would sometimes see the well-to-do older women wearing bouffant hairdos, prim and proper little gold earrings, and matching purses and pumps. Many of these women had just come from a meeting with their interior decorator or a doctor's appointment. Other shoppers spent their days in volunteer jobs, and they would show up to grab groceries for dinner or a late afternoon coffee. Many end up at the deli counter, with its array of prepared meals like brisket, fried chicken, fish, chili, gourmet salads, veggies, and fruit dishes. Why cook?

Gelson's bakery is divine. Chocolate, lemon, carrot, and fluffy vanilla cakes speak to me through the glass counter, and I hear conspiratorial whispers from the homemade cookies and cup-cakes, too. Their breads are plentiful and fresh out of the oven. There is also the forbidden alligator cake, full of caramel and pecans, laced with white frosting.

On occasion, I have seen a food donation truck in the parking lot, and I wouldn't be surprised to learn that Gelson's donates their leftover food to help the homeless. When I am in the mood to make a dessert rather than to buy one, I make a divine and easy white chocolate salad. I got this recipe years ago from a Beverly Hills High School extension class for adults. It's simple, delicious, and refreshing after a heavy meal.

WHITE CHOCOLATE SALAD

INGREDIENTS
- 3 pints of strawberries, blueberries, raspberries, and kiwi
- 3/4 cup white chocolate chips
- 2/3 cup shelled pistachios, chopped pecans, or unsalted macadamias
- 1 cup of whipping cream
- 3 tbsp sugar
- 2 egg yolks
- 1 tsp vanilla

DIRECTIONS
- Bring cream to a slow boil, then remove from stove
- Beat eggs and sugar in a bowl
- Whisk hot cream into the egg mixture slowly (or you will get scrambled eggs)
- Return to pan and cook till thickened, stirring constantly; stir in vanilla
- Can be chilled in the fridge, but sometimes I like this warm
- Combine fruit and nuts in wine glasses. Top with custard and serve (6 servings)

Fortunately, Gelson's produce department is adjacent to the bakery, serving as a reminder that you should be buying healthy produce. Refined white flour, sugar, and oil are indulgences that you should only eat occasionally. I've found that the healthier you eat, the less you crave the unhealthy stuff.

The checkout staff are very friendly, and everyone knows our family members. I've seen many staff members get married and have children, and now they like to show me pictures of their families and celebrations. Before you know it, their kids are graduating from high school and that makes you really feel old. Suddenly, I realized that I was becoming my mother when engaging with the employees. It's a nice thing to do because it connects us with people who are part of our lives. My brother taught me to address a service person by their name, and I always do this when ordering in a restaurant. Good manners go along with integrity.

Gelson's takes care of their employees. They get great benefits and most stay until retirement. Jerry, an older man in the deli department, always waited on me and he would typically flirt with the women, right up until his retirement. It felt like he was everyone's mildly naughty grandpa.

My Mom loved watching the Dodgers, and she instructed everyone not to call her during a game. Why? Because she was smitten with Sean Green, a young Dodger baseball player. After Mom passed, I was talking to a beautiful young woman and her precocious daughter one day at the Gelson's coffee bar. We connected while we talked about family life. After a long time, she told me her husband was Sean Green. I couldn't believe this. What were my chances of this happening? There are no accidents. I looked skyward and smiled up at my mom. Whenever we meet now, we hug and sometimes chat about child rearing as we sip our iced tea.

It is always nice to meet a friend or acquaintance at Gelson's, but I choose to sip my iced tea alone in the coffee bar whenever I am troubled about an issue in my life. I think, process, pause, and repeat. Often, a solution will come to mind, and this is why it is my special place. I have visions of two of me, facing each other at the coffee bar with the pros and cons of the issue. It's my miniature bipolar moment; patient Lynda and therapist Lynda going back and forth like a tennis match. We all need that strong voice within.

When it is storming outside and you crave meat loaf and mashed potatoes; when you are reminded of the current state of our world; when your toilet overflows; when you must go for a root canal or you have a tiff with your spouse, you always know that you can stop for one more iced tea at Gelson's, where everyone really does know your name.

LOU'S FAVORITE MEAT LOAF

INGREDIENTS
- 1 tbsp butter
- ¾ cup minced green onion
- ¾ cup minced white onion
- ½ cup minced carrot
- ½ cup minced celery
- ¼ cup minced red and green pepper
- 2 tbsp minced garlic
- 1 tsp salt and 1 tsp pepper
- ½ tsp cayenne pepper
- ½ tsp nutmeg
- ½ tsp cumin
- 3 beaten eggs
- ½ cup of ketchup or Heinz Chili Sauce
- ½ cup half and half
- 1 ½ lbs. ground beef
- ½ lb. ground pork
- ¾ cup breadcrumbs or almond flour

DIRECTIONS
- Preheat oven to 350 degrees F
- Heat butter in skillet over medium heat, add green onion, white onion, carrots, celery, red and green pepper, and garlic — stir often for 10 minutes — let cool
- Combine all the spices to this mixture
- Stir in half and half, the ketchup or chili sauce, meats, eggs, and flour
- Mix well and form into loaf pan; bake 45-50 minutes, let stand for ten minutes, pour off grease
- Top with additional sauce and 1 tbsp brown sugar if desired during the last 10 minute of baking

CHAPTER 9

LAUREN

"There is something in the nature of tea that leads us into the
world of quiet contemplation of life."

— *Lin Yutang*

Memorial Day has been one of my happiest days of the year
and one of the most devastating. I had married my husband in Las Vegas on Memorial Day after a whirlwind courtship,
never regretting my decision. But on Memorial Day 2008, we
lost our beloved daughter Lauren.

At age 26, Lauren was living in New York and working as a
Ford international model. Enjoying the pulse of the city, she was
living an exotic life of travel while also enrolled at New York
University to become a certified life coach. Even better, she had
met her true love.

Lauren and Alex had been dating for almost a year and
planned to make a life together. She loved him, and she had always loved Central Park. Her poetic spirit favored the movie *Autumn in New York*. In that film, Richard Gere and Wynona Ryder

had the kind of chemistry that mirrored the magical connection between Lauren and Alex.

They were having a blissful day, enjoying a romantic weekend. But as they were jogging in Central Park, she abruptly went into cardiac arrest due to an undiscovered heart condition. Alex stayed by her side, and I can only imagine the terror that he felt, as he experienced the whole tragedy from beginning to end.

David and I had always looked forward to the Memorial Day weekend and celebrating our anniversary. We did so every year. It was our 30-year anniversary, and we were preparing to drive down the coast for an oceanfront brunch. But then, one phone call changed our lives forever.

2008 had already been a difficult year for many Americans, as the country was entering one of the worst recessions. We lost a good part of our nest egg due to the collapse of the real estate market; we were not alone since this was a national phenomenon. However, nothing prepared us for the awful news from the ER doctor at Lenox Hill Hospital.

Everything became a blur after that, as my consciousness left my physical body. I had to stop screaming, pull it together, and call my extended family. I don't remember very much but I recall the Newport Beach police officers knocking on our doors to check on us after they received the news from New York. Within hours, our house was filled with neighbors, friends, and family. Many instantly flew in to support us and be by our sides.

It was a moment of not even recognizing life as I had known it. It was my dark turning point, plunging into the abyss for what would be a long time. I was entering a room in a house of darkness and grieving. It was also a life experience that has defined who I am today.

My subsequent spiritual journey, with tea in hand, forced me to explore and examine the meaning of life. I had to surrender to the steps of acceptance, repair, and resilience. I needed to learn to have grit and to lean in, facing that rainbow of emotions. There were no short cuts. Jamie Anderson describes the essence of grieving this way:

> *"Grief, I've learned, is really just love. It's all the love you want to give but cannot. All that unspent love gathers up in the corners of your eyes, the lump in your throat, and in that hollow part of your chest. Grief is just love with no place to go."*

My family was broken, and it was a slow process to resume to any kind of normal living. For our other daughter Ashlie, it meant the loss of her best friend and mentor. She had just graduated from college and was starting a new job at a prestigious advertising firm. Today, as a devoted wife and mother, she often honors Lauren by sharing sister stories with her two babies. Lauren would be very proud of her sister, and I know her fairy dust continues to grace Ashlie with love and support.

Lauren was at her happiest with Alex, so in love with him and her life. A sense of peace and serenity was with her that whole year, despite the discomfort of having her wisdom teeth extracted. Just a few months prior to her passing, she came home to see the dentist; I took care of her throughout her painful recuperation. It was my pleasure to feed her soup and stay up with her during the night as any mama bear would, of course.

She was a trouper, toughing it out with only Tylenol to manage the pain. Lauren was eight years sober, and she embraced the gifts of sobriety wholeheartedly. Her near-death alcohol poisoning experience and hospitalization had been a wake-up call at age eighteen.

That episode had occurred on Memorial Day in the adult playground atmosphere of Lake Havasu, where boating and bar parties were ubiquitous. After she returned home and confessed to this horrific ordeal, she participated in a two-week outpatient rehab, and then joined AA after completion. It's eerie that she almost died on that Memorial Day, and yet she had eight additional years to become the person God intended her to be.

In defiance of the grim statistics about relapses for alcoholism, Lauren never wavered with her sobriety, and attended daily meetings. She spoke out about her journey and became one of the most requested AA speakers in Southern California and New York.

This indeed was her calling, much more so than modeling. Her wisdom and compassion helped thousands of recovering addicts. Her spiritual depths were profound, with holistic habits of healthy nutrition, metaphysical books, and intellectual lectures. She acquired a deep sense of purpose and a dedication to giving back, which aligned her soul. She was on a path and a mission, knowing that her modeling days no longer fulfilled her passion.

Lauren dealt with depression and anxiety, but with kindness and a productive daily schedule to navigate the periods of darkness. These episodes became less frequent as she aged, but it was hard work exercising that muscle of perseverance. I watched this transformation, rooting her on and admiring her dedication to not only take care of herself, but to help others.

Yes, she was ahead of the game, but Lauren never forgot her early days of struggling. By sharing her vulnerable side, Lauren leveraged her past experiences to help others with similar challenges. It took genuine courage to be so openly vulnerable. She was a role model who provided others the chance to learn and grow. Her generous and estimable acts in helping others filled her with gratitude; this was her opportunity to make a difference in the world. She left this earth as an old soul.

Our grief was deep and unrelenting. David and I could not leave the house for days. He lost twenty pounds and I worried that he was going to die. Our house was filled with neighbors and friends, but when they left my home was filled with broken hearts and tears.

We finally stepped out to Gelson's coffee bar. As soon as we entered the store, the manager and almost every checkout clerk sprinted toward us to form a group huddle of hugs. Meanwhile, long queues of people were lining the aisles because no one was attending the cash registers. It looked like a scene from the day before Thanksgiving. This is community.

The compassion from friends and neighbors was overwhelming. My friends, Trudy and Kathy, checked on us every day. My local Peeps, Kelli, Lorraine, and Lori dragged me out to lunch monthly. My yoga teacher, Ell, had nothing but spiritual compassion for me and walked me through the bi-weekly yoga classes. A Los Angeles newspaper article about Lauren's life, accomplishments, and her passing was posted up in the coffee bar. Lauren meant a lot to our community.

When I was teaching high school, Lauren visited my school and many others to speak to students about the gifts of sobriety. She told her story about the dangers of excessive drinking and drug use. She showed them the blueprint of how she nearly lost her life.

Lauren's beauty always helped her get everyone's attention, but her mission was to share her vulnerability and explain that pain and suffering cannot be solved through alcohol and drugs. Many in the audience entered the auditorium flippant, but left crying from the impact of the reality she described; sharing an authentic life was her mission.

She lived exactly eight years from that dark Memorial Day, and perhaps that was God's plan for her time on earth. She is dearly missed by all of us, and I think often about how she could have helped many more broken people.

I found this poem (often attributed to Jorge Luis Borges) in Lauren's journal. Its message about self-reliance, resilience, and the power of love is ideal to share with young women.

Comes the Dawn

After a while you learn the subtle difference
Between holding a hand and chaining a soul
And you learn that love doesn't mean leaning
And company doesn't mean security

And you begin to understand that kisses aren't contracts
And presents aren't promises

And you begin to accept your defeats
With your head held high and your eyes open
With the grace of a woman, not the grief of a child

You learn to build your roads
On today because tomorrow's ground
Is too uncertain for plans, and futures have
A way of falling down in midflight

After a while you learn that even sunshine
Burns if you get too much
So you plant your own garden and decorate
Your own soul, instead of waiting
For someone to bring you flowers

And you learn that you can really endure,
That you really are strong

And you really do have worth
And you learn and learn ... and you learn
With every goodbye you learn.

There was no defibrillator available for someone to help Lauren when she went down; it could have saved her life. The Rescue Heart Foundation, created by the angelic Angela Howell-Eagerly, generously donated two defibrillators to New York

Central Park in memory of Lauren Zussman so that joggers can have a lifeline in the event of heart failure.

On so many levels, our girl did not die in vain; her angel dust continues to touch others. Three newborns have been named after her, including her niece, in honor of a life well-lived. As Norman Cousins stated: "If something comes to life in others because of you, then you have made an approach to immortality."

I miss our tea parties in bed. I miss our routine of eating salmon and grilled vegetables. Oh, how she loved to eat, and it was a pleasure to feed her. I miss her laughter. I miss her mane of chestnut brown hair flowing down her back. I miss her unassuming inner and outer beauty. She was a gift. She was Lauren.

I wrote about Lauren every day in the garden for months, chronicling her transition from a troubled teen to a wise and fruitful woman. The process was cathartic and became a book. *Throw Me the Rope: A Memoir on Loving Lauren* was widely read and warmly received. After an excerpt was printed in the Los Angeles Times, I received hundreds of e-mails from other parents who had lost children. All I could do was to respond with my hope that their joyous memories of their child would overshadow the darkness of their passing.

For anyone who is grieving, any kind of forward activity helps to mitigate the pain and suffering. These steps worked for me and may be useful to you, too:

1. Self-compassion! Feel what you feel and name it: fear, anger, sadness, depression, anxiety, stress, loneliness, misery, lost, heartbroken, etc. Write about it in a journal, preferably in the morning. Everyone grieves in their own way, so do what feels right to you. If you can, go outside to your yard, patio or balcony. The sun and vitamin D help the brain to process.

2. Try to find a way to be with nature. Try walking even if it's only a block. Go to the ocean, a lake, or river. The water is soothing. Invest in a fountain. I am greeted by mine every morning and it begins my day. Sit at a park or any tranquil setting.

3. Don't be afraid to reach out for help. There are many ways to find guidance during this time. Religious leaders, therapist, mentors, and support groups help with the grieving process.

4. Make small and long-term goals, starting out with baby steps. I found comfort in familiar and satisfying tasks like making soup, planting a garden, organizing the home, or focusing on a new hobby. Religious and community centers are everywhere. Returning to yoga was a key factor in the beginning of my healing.

5. Do something to honor your loved one. Go to a soup kitchen and help. Write a poem, volunteer at a senior center, or read to children at your local school.

6. Lastly, understand there will be waves of emotions. Surf the waves and when you see joy again (you will), jump on it!

To grasp the complex issues of life and death, I maintained a daily routine of tea in my garden while reading inspirational and spiritual books. Lauren is with me every single day, if only in my mind while I drink my tea. Tea is good. Tea is nurturing. Tea can give us hope. Life can be good again.

Immortality

Do not stand
By my grave, and weep.
I am not there,
I do not sleep—
I am the thousand winds that blow
I am the diamond glints in snow
I am the sunlight on ripened grain,
I am the gentle, autumn rain.
As you awake with morning's hush,
I am the swift, up-flinging rush
Of quiet birds in circling flight,
I am the day transcending night.
Do not stand
By my grave, and cry—
I am not there,
I did not die.

- Clare Harner, 1934

GARDEN TEA FOR MEDITATION
(NO NEED TO BAKE)

- Place a Lavender Jasmine tea bag in 8 ounces of hot water for 5 minutes in your best teacup
- Remove bag and add a teaspoon of honey
- Enjoy with shortbread cookies or lemon thins
- Dipping allowed

CHAPTER 10

THE HISTORY OF TEAS, RITUALS, AND DAILY PLEASURES

"There are few hours in life more agreeable than the hour dedicated to the ceremony known as afternoon tea."

— *Henry James*

The history of tea is long and complex, spreading across multiple cultures over thousands of years. Some accounts suggest that tea originated in the Yunnan region of China during the Shang dynasty (1600-1046 BC) as a medicinal drink. An early credible record of tea drinking dates to the third century AD in a medical text written by Hua Too.

Tea containers have been discovered in tombs dating back to the Han dynasty (206 BC - 220 AD). By the time of the Tang dynasty (618-906 AD), tea was fully established as the national drink of China.

Tea was first introduced to Europe through Portuguese priests and merchants in India and Lebanon, beginning in 1569 or earlier. In 1610, the Dutch brought tea to Northern Europe, and drinking tea became popular in Britain during the 17th century. The British encouraged tea production and consumption in India to compete with the Chinese monopoly on tea.

According to *The Story of Tea* by Mary Lou and Robert Heiss, tea began as a medicinal drink. Tea drinking became a ritual when people began consuming tea for pleasure in Southwest China. Tea has played a significant role in Asian culture for centuries as a staple beverage, a curative, and a status symbol. The theories around tea ritual origins are often religious or royal in nature.

By the sixth century, tea use had spread to Japan, where it became a drink for the religious classes. Japanese priests encourage the growth of tea plants; seeds were brought from China and cultivated in Japan. Green tea became a staple among cultured people and the Buddhist priesthood. Production grew and tea became increasingly accessible, though it remained a privilege enjoyed mostly by the upper classes. The formal tea ceremony was introduced to Japan from China in the 15th century by Buddhists as a semi-religious social custom.

In Korea, the daily tea rite was a common daytime ceremony for the aristocracy. The "special tea rite" was reserved for occasions such as welcoming visiting foreigners or royal weddings. Green tea is often regarded as the purest type. In Viet Nam, tea houses are retreats where lotus tea and jasmine tea are served.

After the pleasure of drinking tea spread to Europe, the British became enamored of this magical elixir. The afternoon tea ritual is firmly established in most parts of the United Kingdom. Tea drinkers in the cosmopolitan cities of America have embraced the ritual of tea drinking, as tea houses here have flourished since the 1970s.

My sober friends have turned to tea. People with serious illnesses have turned to tea. Medicinal teas have been known for centuries, and countless studies and professional health journals have documented the health benefits of drinking tea, and particularly green tea. How does green tea differ from black?

For black tea, the leaves are fermented, which triggers an oxidation process. This reaction causes the leaves to turn dark and allow the flavors to intensify. Green tea is more raw, lighter in color, and has less caffeine. Both types are beneficial to one's health. The varieties of tea differ mainly in how much the leaves are permitted to oxidize.

It's important to distinguish herbal teas from the "true" teas that are made from the leaves of the tea plant *camellia sinensis*. True teas can be black, white, green, or oolong, but they all come from this plant, and they all have caffeine. True tea is not only a wonderful drink, but also genuinely sustainable; leaves are plucked every 15-30 days from a plant that is never uprooted.

Herbal teas are made from flowers, herbs, and other vegetable sources – but not from the camellia sinensis leaves. They typically have no caffeine. Like the true teas, herbal teas are tasty relaxing beverages that frequently offer a variety of health benefits.

Research has validated tea's long-standing reputation for supporting physical and mental health. Tea contains polyphenols that can mitigate damaging free radicals. Green tea is regarded as more beneficial than black tea, but both have anti-aging properties. Studies have shown a significant decrease in the risk of hypertension, diabetes, cardiovascular disease, and strokes for persons who drink 3-5 cups per day of tea.

Tea can sharpen your mental focus, improve your mood, and elevate your physical performance. Both green and black teas contain less caffeine than coffee while providing L-theanine, an amino acid shown to promote a state of calm awareness. I believe that it can genuinely relax the mind to help you be joyfully present.

Tea has an anti-anxiety effect and is often helpful with insomnia. I know this from experience, especially when I am feeling a lot of stress. Teas consumption increases dopamine, can help moderate blood pressure, and may indeed lower the risk of certain cancers.

Tea can be a tonic to reduce fatigue, irritability, and food cravings. Hot or iced, tea is a delicious and healthy drink that is an indispensable part of my daily diet. At Gelson's, my favorite is the Paradise tea. I can enjoy about thirty-two ounces of that delicious tropical-flavored tea daily, and later in the day switch to my home-brewed teas. I was rarely sick when I taught school, avoiding both colds and the flu. The classrooms, learning labs, and my office were busy environments loaded with people and of course viruses and germs.

Drinking tea can, of course, fulfill your daily hydration needs. Green tea, oolong, Yerba mate, goji, and kola nut teas have a type of flavonoid called catechins that are reputed to boost metabolism. Kava, ashwagandha, passionflower, hops, lemon balm, valerian, chamomile, and lavender teas can help with anxiety and sleepless nights. Loose tea is more potent than tea in bags, but both kinds contain folic acid, a B vitamin that's important for red blood cell formation and healthy cell growth.

I have been making cold tea by combining Earl Grey tea with jasmine tea, and it is divine over ice, ideal with meals. Refrigerated bottled unsweetened black tea is my favorite go-to when I don't want to make my own, and I enjoy it in peach or raspberry flavor (be careful about which additives are used in artificial or natural flavors). I don't know why, but this bottled tea gives me a more intense brain buzz than coffee does; I think more clearly and I have more energy.

I try not to eat after six o'clock. To help me stick to that, after dinner I drink fresh mint tea to ward off hunger. Some doctors endorse fresh basil tea to support the immune system, so I drink that when my allergies kick up. It's important to make the tea with fresh sweet basil, the familiar kind used in Italian cooking. Be sure not to confuse fresh basil with products marketed as "holy basil," for which there is not yet sufficient research to support any related health benefits.

Valerian tea can be a mild sedative; so much so, in fact that I cannot drink it. However, many rely on it for getting a good night's rest. Check with your doctor and see if its benefits outweigh the risks of side effects and drug interactions. Chamomile and lavender tea both enjoy a reputation as helpful in relief for fatigue and depression, and now it's become trendy to drink lemon balm and licorice tea for immune system support. Keep in mind, finding your go-to tea is a process of trial and error.

Some teas can be detrimental to your health and interfere with your medication or condition. Always check with your doctor to be safe, especially if you are pregnant. The same herbs and plants used in some teas are also base for many drugs and may cause more harm than good.

With that note of caution, I'm happy to report only positive tea experiences. For me, teas have been both calming and energizing. And that makes sense, according to Joyce Maina, director of the *Cambridge Tea Consultancy*. She notes that the caffeine is a natural stimulant, but the L-theanine amino acid relaxes the mind. What other product can do both at once? I feel that my daily consumption of tea has improved my health and certainly the function of my immune system.

From the British Isles to Southeast Asia, tea is the daily ritual in many cultures. People rely on tea as a key component of their physical and spiritual health; I've done so too, for decades. Although I do enjoy a good cup of fresh brewed coffee every morning, it is teatime for me for the rest of the day.

I embrace tea as a definitive act of simplicity and inner peace. It is the essence of social connections. It is a ritual, a meditation, and a cleansing of one's mind. Tea is a simple and easy path to an almost spiritual experience. Tea offers comfort, promotes clarity, enhances my mood, provides hydration, and gives me a sense of well-being. Tea is hygienic, cleansing my body and clearing my throat. My tea ritual – at Gelson's, at home, or out with friends – has always been my healthy addiction.

Sometimes, sipping a cup of tea lets you appreciates your surroundings, and journaling with gratitude is at the top of my list before bedtime. It's just the tea and me during quiet moments, and I love to sink into my soft recliner chair to savor those occasions. I become present; not dwelling on the past or worrying about the future. The complexity of the world and life is on pause. The tea becomes a part of me.

I give tea sets to people as gifts, often with a candle. It's my way of sending love and peace; perhaps the gift of tea is a better message than a gift of wine. Tea is a social event; the ritual of drinking tea is so wonderful when catching up with a good friend.

We Americans are finally catching on to what the Chinese and Brits have known for centuries. High tea is a fantastic way to ease into late afternoon, alone or with a friend. There are a growing number of restaurants and tea houses where you can enjoy a formal tea ceremony, often with something sweet to munch on. Here is my favorite recipe for delicious blueberry buttermilk scones to accompany your tea of choice. It's quick and easy. Enjoy!

BLUEBERRY BUTTERMILK SCONES

INGREDIENTS
- 2 cups buttermilk baking mix (often sold as pancake or waffle mix)
- 3 tbsp sugar
- 1/3 cup (3/4 stick) salted butter, softened
- 1 cup of organic frozen or fresh blueberries
- 3/4 cup milk
- Lemon curd or fresh unsalted butter, for serving

DIRECTIONS
- Preheat oven to 400 degrees F
- Add baking mix, sugar, and butter in a large bowl
- Add milk; mix to form 12 balls
- Place on a greased cooking sheet or in a muffin tin
- Bake on center rack 15-18 minutes or until golden brown
- Serve with lemon curd or butter, enjoy with ginger tea

CHAPTER 11

THE COFFEE BAR REGULARS

"You want to be where you can see
Our troubles are all the same
You want to be where everybody knows your name"
— *Cheers theme, lyrics by Gary Portnoy
and Judy Hart-Angelo*

I have met so many fascinating characters at Gelson's coffee bars throughout the years. Like me, these folks are regulars because it's their retreat. Some are my friends, some are frankly annoying, and some are just fascinating or quirky. Let's examine a few thumbnails of the Gelson's cast of characters, beginning with my favorite, Bernie. The names have been changed to respect their privacy.

Bernie may be the most memorable of the people I have known or befriended at Gelson's. As mentioned before, he was the sweetest senior gentleman, well into his nineties. Bernie is gone now but I think of him often, because he was always so wise, positive, and genuinely interested in my family. In his modest way, Bernie lived a very full and rich ninety-six years on this planet.

Shelly is a mature and insightful woman who was raised in Chicago, as I was. She is genuine, sincere, and skilled in maintaining a dignified look. Because of our shared Chicago backgrounds, we quickly found a familiarity that I sometimes find elusive with west coast natives. I think that folks from Chicago share values and put an emphasis on education over money. I loved my time in California, but I never fully adjusted to people's fanaticism about cars and the urge to display wealth. However, I do love designer handbags.

Todd is at the coffee bar every time I visit. By my observation, he is in his fifties, losing his hair, and he suffers from obsessive compulsive disorder. The coffee bar is his home for many hours; he will frequently leave and then come back for refills. He spends his time at the bar continuously counting his one-dollar bills, and he does not speak to anyone. One can only imagine the troubles in his mind, but the coffee bar is his refuge.

I am wonderfully amused by two senior ladies that I met 20 years ago; everyone calls them Twin A and Twin B. One is divorced and the other is widowed, and now they are inseparable. These identical twins live together, and they are a hoot at the coffee bar. Some cable network could easily produce a reality show around these two charming old birds. The mirror-image extroverted fashionistas, adorned with knock-off designer purses, command attention as soon as they reach the bar. The Twins are social climbers, and they will strike up a conversation to obtain a phone number from any fellow patron whose clothes or jewelry make the impression of wealth and status.

Bambi is a young sweet blonde mother sporting a ponytail, baseball cap, and yoga clothes. She meets her friends and neighbors at Gelson's after dropping her kids off at school. There is always a table of young mothers chatting and enjoying their coffee or tea before resuming all their chores for the day.

Nicole is a skinny vegan who feels a calling to police the people eating meat in the coffee bar. She is in her fifties, but dresses like a young hippie in shorts, sneakers, and a t-shirt. She (probably) means well but she is unabashedly vocal in protesting against people eating meat at any time. I saw her challenge a man who was about to bite into his roast beef sandwich.

Marvin is a fifty-something single doctor who always wears his doctor scrubs with a stethoscope to attract young single girls. Topped with a mismatched toupee, he will often ask if anyone can fix him up with single girls, despite his failures with dating apps and services like J-Date. Marvin totes a car magazine in case he needs to show a cute patron a picture of his Porsche or Bentley. Marvin represents a caricature of all the worst Californian traits.

Steven and Maggie bring politics to the bar. Steven is a Republican and an attorney, always ranting about the news being broadcast by CNN on the screen above the coffee bar. The Wall Street Journal is always on his table as he drinks one coffee after another. A bit hyper but never embarrassed, Steven will converse with anyone who will listen to his soap box rants.

Maggie is also an attorney, but a liberal. Maggie is a mature woman who is passionate about grass root organizations. She drinks her tea and works on her laptop every day, such that the coffee bar is her office. When Maggie and Steven are sitting next to each other, one of them will frequently move to a different chair because they have engaged in some heated discussions over the years.

Rosie is a Gelson's staff member in charge of the floral arrangements, filling the orders for sometimes difficult patrons. This hearty woman, with a stunning shock of red hair, brings good cheer and her jolly sense of humor to the customers when she takes her break in the coffee bar. She adds lightness to any group of patrons, and she is ready to laugh at about anything.

All of these characters have a distinct personality worth observing. The psychological, emotional, and social well-being has an impact on every aspect of one's life. Positive mental health essentially deals with life's everyday challenges. Diet, sleep, exercise, spirituality, and socialization are at the top of my list to maintain some sort of continuous normalcy. Sometimes when the waves get rocky, I have to pull down the shades and retreat for twenty-four hours. This too is healthy.

The older we get, the harder it is to make new friends. It is even harder to make new friends when our children get older. Joining interest groups such as investment clubs, classes in the arts, culinary classes, etc. can present new opportunities to meet people of like kind. There are hiking meets, yoga classes, exercise classes and the list goes on and on. It is best to stay active and be open to new beginnings.

I think as we age, we gravitate to healthier relationships knowing what to attract and what to avoid. I shy away from drama queens and negative people. At one time in my life, I let too many people in with unhealthy agendas or personality disorders. My eyes are open and when I bond with a friend who is truly a friend, I keep that person forever. If you have five people who you can count on, who make you laugh, who are there when the chips are down, then you are a lucky individual.

There have been mentors in my life who have made a profound impact on my life. My mother for one, but others who have had my best interest at heart. I try to take these life lessons and pass the wisdom on to others.

The world is facing incredible challenges and without dwelling on the negative, we all need to encourage change with some optimism. I really think it begins with our community and perhaps the positive effect we have with each other can branch out to other areas. I think that is why I loved being a special education educator. I was helping little souls with the extra challenges in life. When two souls meet in the middle whether its adult to child, or adult to adult, then it is the true reason we are here. Isn't it? Add a sweet and a cup of tea and you have made your own little nirvana.

I have made some great friends at Gelson's, but I appreciate the whole variety of characters that are regulars in that space. The world isn't always easy or perfect, but we can be at peace with the world as we find it. Do you know what helps bring people together, as much as coffee or tea? Cookies! Here's a hack on chocolate chip cookies that makes them healthier and even better tasting.

PUMPKIN CHOCOLATE CHIP COOKIES

INGREDIENTS
- 1 17.5 oz. package gingerbread, oatmeal, or sugar cookie mix
- 1/2 stick butter, softened
- 1 15-oz. can of pumpkin
- 1 egg
- 1 package of dark chocolate chips
- 1 can vanilla or cream cheese frosting (optional)

DIRECTIONS
- Preheat oven to 385 degrees F
- Ignore package directions; mix all the ingredients in a large bowl
- Use a wooden spoon to drop balls of dough onto lightly greased baking sheet (makes about 40 cookies; you may need two baking sheets)
- Bake at 385 for 12 minutes; then flip cookies over. Be careful, they are very soft at that point
- Bake for another 8-12 minutes, before bottoms get too dark
- As soon as they are cool, flip them over again so that the bottoms don't get soggy
- Add icing after they are cool
- Store in an open container; if you wrap them or enclose them, they get too soft due to the high moisture content

CHAPTER 12

HEALTH AND AGING

"A cup of tea is an excuse to share great
thoughts with great minds."

— *Cristina Re*

I never thought about being in my sixties. How did this happen? My mother said to me many years ago, "I don't know what happened, but I rolled over one morning, and I was sixty-five years old." It seems like yesterday when I was full of energy, wearing bell bottom jeans, and sporting long, black, thick, straight hair. The passage of time was irrelevant as we lived life in the moment; carefree, innocent, and full of gusto.

This year I noticed my joints are a bit achy, my hair is a bit thinner, and I think I shrunk by an inch. I need reading glasses; one day, I kept calling the wrong number because I couldn't read the print. The third time I called this poor woman, I apologized profusely, and I finally fetched my glasses.

The weight does creep up, and if you don't keep moving, your joints become stiff. New wrinkles appear in the mirror, and you start to look like someone you once knew. Only as you age do you have to pay attention to keeping your balance; I once fell over while putting on my pants. Now I sit for that daily chore. My bones snap, crackle, and pop. Sometimes, like the tin man, I need oil.

I'm drawn to news about the latest disease or what new vitamin we need to prevent horrible maladies. Of course, I've learned that I shouldn't research any symptoms on the internet; the literature will convince you that you are dying.

When you go for a regular check-up, it's largely about looking for cancer and taking a slew of tests. I won't repeat the mistake of going in for medical testing at the end of the week, because the results are delayed over the weekend. I know the dread you feel when the technician says "we need to take a few more slides" of your potential cancer that is lurking there. Of course, she doesn't say that directly; she blames it on the film.

Still, we must be active and positive. The health of the mind and the body are intertwined. I love taking cooking classes, reading healthy food blogs, and finding delectable recipes. Life is more interesting if you keep stimulated with things like art history, writing, music, a new language, or attending a lecture. Social interaction extends your life expectancy, and that is another reason why I love going to Gelson's. My peeps are there and it's a good time to catch up with friends.

Retirement gives us the freedom to play like the child we once were. I admire the people who paint because that activity can be meditative and relaxing. Remember the excitement when the teacher said it was time to have art in our classrooms? Art and music elevate our lives. Music is indispensable to my day; it's my drug-free antidepressant at home or out in the world.

Volunteering is good food for the soul. More than once, on Lauren's birthday my husband and I have worked in a soup kitchen to honor our late daughter, because it's something she did regularly. I've also enjoyed working with foster teens and I learn something new each time. And we shouldn't overlook the value of the unconditional love we get from our pets. Cowboy is still my number one dog, and all he wants is a little turkey and a lot of love.

For me, visual beauty in the home is important for a tranquil state of mind. I like elaborate landscaping and well-constructed furniture. Smartly designed furnishings and accessories can spark joy; I love purses, handbags, shoes, and my comfortable organic mattress. It's not a contradiction, I think, to say that I prefer simplicity, but I recognize too that jewelry is a form of art and beauty.

While clothes have never been my passion, I acknowledge the importance of clothing in daily life. My low-bar goal is to look nice and somewhat put together. For most occasions I can get by with just a few basic articles of clothing.

At this point in my life, I am traveling less and relaxing more. Decorating, gardening, and improving our home gives me a sense of contentment. In California, my small castle with a serene garden near the Pacific Ocean gave me a peaceful feeling, especially with the fountain flowing and the sound of the trickling water. This is a simple happiness that derives from the wisdom of age, contentment, and being comfortable in one's own skin.

Books, magazines, and a good conversation with a neighbor make the day complete. Classical or New Age music in the background enhances my aura, even when the weather turns dark and gloomy. Yet, I love when it rains! It's a good time to light a fire, read a good book, and sip tea. I lean back daily in my plush recliner to read or meditate. Now I know why old people sit in rocking chairs.

One advantage of aging is you can finally hear what you want to hear and see what you want to see. You no longer care about what other people think of you and you can reinvent yourself (over and over), if only for a day at a time. Aging well is giving yourself the freedom to be who you were meant to be.

My husband is a decade older than me, and he is still my prince. David is a very loving man. When I complain it is cold in the middle of the night, he will get up to put socks on my feet. This man always brings my morning coffee, and he will make eggs and toast for me if I request. We had incredible passion in the early days and have played many roles throughout the years. Sometimes we are lovers, sometimes brother and sister, sometimes father and mother— and it is all okay. We roll with the punches in life and have always been a team. I overheard him tell a friend one day that he is going down with the ship. I guess I'm the ship.

David has retained his good looks and his full head of hair while keeping his weight down through daily exercise. He survived melanoma thirty years ago, a misdiagnosed brain tumor from a leading neurologist, a heart valve replacement, the MGM fire in Las Vegas, the ups and downs of the economy, and the incomprehensible loss of our daughter, Lauren. He is my hero.

We both have a sense of humor that keeps us in the light, even during dark times. After my doctor told me that my blood test revealed high levels of arsenic, I told him "That's strange, because my husband just took out a two-million-dollar life insurance policy on me." His face turned pale, but I then told him I was just kidding.

When I came home, I told my husband my arsenic levels are dangerously high, and my doctor had to report this to the police as possible poisoning. I said that the police are coming over later in the day to investigate. His face turned pale, and then I told him I was just kidding. I'm glad that his sense of humor is on the same level as mine!

Sex is good, sex is healthy. It brings a couple closer together at any age. However, when you're hot you're hot, and when you're not, you're not. Many of my female friends are at the opposite ends of the spectrum about sex; some say they can't get enough, while others describe it as a chore. While doing the deed, one friend of mine thinks about her grocery shopping list, unbeknownst to her partner. She imagines the aisles as she scans the store; oatmeal, pasta, yogurt, "oh baby," eggs, potatoes, bananas, "oh baby."

Our local farmers market sells incredible crumb-topped blueberry pies; David and I bought one and lathered pure whipped cream on top for an afternoon delight with (you guessed it) a cup of tea. For our pleasure we're happy to substitute sweets for sex. Joy is where you find it!

Women and men are so different, and they experience intimacy differently. Especially in my generation, women cook for their men while men fill up their wives' gas tanks. Women have sex when they don't really feel like it; men pick up the dog doo in the yard. Men mow lawns; women do laundry. Men lie that the meal was delicious; women moan from pleasure, faking orgasm. It all works out.

I often feel that men were not meant to be psychologically sensitive to the female's feelings. That is why we ladies have girlfriends; we need other humans who listen and understand us. Men crave food, sex, and the remote control. You won't find them in the psychology aisle at Barnes & Noble.

Sex and food, fundamental sources of pleasure. While Gelson's has wonderful organic meats, I aim for salads, veggies, and fruits. I target things like organic yogurt and free-range eggs as part of a simple whole food diet. I don't tolerate meat well at night, which may be another sign of old age. If I do indulge, ginger tea must follow with a brownie.

KATHERINE HEPBURN'S BROWNIES

INGREDIENTS
- 1/2 cup cocoa
- 1 stick of butter
- 2 eggs
- 1 cup sugar
- 1/4 cup flour
- 1 cup broken-up walnuts or pecans
- 1 tsp vanilla
- Pinch salt

DIRECTIONS
- Preheat oven to 325 degrees F
- Melt butter in saucepan with cocoa and stir until smooth. Remove from heat and allow to cool for a few minutes
- Whisk in eggs, one at a time. Stir in vanilla
- In separate bowl, combine sugar, flour, nuts, and salt. Add to the cocoa-butter mixture. Stir until just combined
- Pour into a greased 8 X 8 square pan. Bake 40 minutes. Do not overbake, it should be gooey. Let cool and cut into bars
- Enjoy with earl grey tea

My husband and I have opposite taste in movies. He loves films with action, adventure, blood, and guts. I prefer dramas featuring strong lead characters with a good story arc, documentaries, or a fresh comedy with iconic stars like Diane Keaton or Meryl Streep. I've never met a man who watches movies on the *Lifetime* network.

What David and I share is a true gift. We have each other's backs, true compassion for the other's physical or mental pain, and we stay present to listen. After the joy of eloping and being madly in love, we felt the excruciating pain of losing a daughter. Weak marriages fall apart after this kind of tragedy, but strong ones thrive with unity.

Aging isn't easy, and humor is our antidote for the woes of the world. David affectionally calls me Poo Poo or Poo Poo Head, which always elicits a laugh from me. He clowns around a lot, especially with our girls. When the girls were young, I was in the kitchen with them when we heard him scream from another room, "I'm Tony the Tiger!" for no apparent reason. It was just absurd enough to make us all laugh hysterically. He would often have these Tourette's-style outbreaks that would put us all in stitches. David would do anything to make the girls laugh.

A joy of aging is that no one can take away the memories of our unit as a family. No one can take away my memories as a mom, wife, or friend. The warm memories overshadow our disappointments. Marriage is there to share the history of the decades if you are lucky enough to have a long-time partner. We used to joke and say, "Whoever leaves has to take the children."

Yes, we bicker, often over driving directions or both of us buying bananas at the same time. We both accuse each other of snoring or who ate the last Oreo, but our love and devotion always rise above our petty scraps. Life can be good, and it's our choosing!

David is predictable, stable, generous, and witty. As I move toward my seventies, I know that these will be our best years. It is like a Saturday morning knowing that the weekend will not last forever. Taking a stroll after dinner, watching a sunset, or sipping iced tea are simple pleasures, so how much should we dwell on our age? You can dye your hair, buy a new outfit, or lose weight, but you can't change your age. However, with age comes wisdom and with wisdom comes peace of mind. It all starts to come together.

Out to dinner a couple of years ago, my husband announced that at age 75, he was super healthy and has never felt better. It was Friday the 13th, a date on which I have experienced many terrible things. I'm not usually superstitious, but his statement was tempting fate.

I awoke that night hearing an animal-like scream, and it was David having a grand mal seizure. At first I thought it was a stroke, but my special education background helped me recognize the seizure. By 2:00 AM, David was surrounded by six paramedics.

When he returned to consciousness, he was taken to the hospital where it was discovered that the episode had resulted from a brain tumor (glioma). My heart was in my stomach, but after several MRIs, the glioma no longer appeared.

We had three months of hell following the initial diagnosis. At one point the medical experts thought it was water on the brain, but that was wrong again. It seemed to be a miracle that this mass had disappeared, and the doctors were baffled. The final determination is that the mass was from a brain infection; encephalitis that mimicked a brain tumor. Three years later, there are no signs of any problems. David is going strong and is so thankful for his health. Whew! Indeed, we appreciate every day with gratitude.

As we age, we seek the people and processes that keep us sane, normal, and as healthy as we can be. I have relied on

Weight Watchers, yoga, meditation, and my Buddhist therapist. Not every day is a wonderful day; there have been times when I've asked friends to drive me to the vet so I can be put down.

I try to practice a healthy and holistic lifestyle daily. This is essential to me and to the people in my social circle. I seek friends who have integrity, intelligence, humor, and compassion. Mental and physical health are foundational to good daily living, and there are no short cuts.

One enduring lesson is that I learned to accept loss and change. With each decade, your resilience can grow. While we must accept reality, never waste a good crisis. If you do have to go through Hell, don't come out empty-handed. Teach others what you have learned, how you persevered, and how you carry on.

About fifteen years ago I noticed my weight was going up, and I needed to do something about it. Looking back, it seems like every decade added ten pounds. It was time to pull it back.

But the battle began long ago. I had spent a very stressful but rewarding ten years when I was teaching, testing, and running intense meetings with parents, teachers, lawyers, and doctors. In those days, I would eat mindlessly. A local bakery would often donate surplus goodies to our teachers' cafeteria. That really did me in. The custard puffed rolls were divine, as well as all of that one-day old pastry assortment. It doesn't help that my husband loves to go out to dinner, where the hidden fat and salt is waiting to destroy my good intentions. By the time I joined Weight Watchers, I had gained an unhealthy twenty pounds.

I still attend the weekly meetings, where I have met some incredible women over the years. I became very close with three women from the Weight Watchers meetings in Newport Beach; we maintain monthly lunchtime get togethers. Kelli came to America from Argentina as a teen, Lori is a single mom from Oklahoma who is raising two adorable children, and Lorraine's family is from England.

We have been there for each other through all the joys and sorrows: births, weddings, deaths, birthdays, and holiday celebrations. We called ourselves The Troublemakers. Perhaps a cable reality show is lurking in there somewhere, *The WW Peeps of Newport Beach*. What the hell, let's enlist Oprah, already an investor and spokesperson for Weight Watchers, to appear in a cameo at our table.

Weight management has been one lifelong challenge, but the mental challenges are often harder than the physical ones. Meditation became a new goal for me; I embraced meditation after struggling with the process of grieving for our late daughter.

After a few years of typical cognitive psychotherapy, I consulted a PHD Buddhist psychotherapist, and it was life changing for me. I had read about Buddhism thirty years earlier. A wise friend gave me *The Tibetan Book of Living and Dying* at a time when I was not ready to experience the richness of staying present with a Buddha on my shoulder. As a Jewish girl with typical garden-variety anxiety, I really had to change my approach to become an observer who is keen to all the feelings – good, bad, and ugly.

Standing still and freezing time was a new experience, and it required patience and practice to master meditation. There are many levels of mastering meditation and being present. I can now recognize my two occasional "friends" who show up at my door without overreacting.

"Oh, here is anxiety and oh, depression just rang my doorbell. Hello, stay awhile and then please leave. I will acknowledge you for a day or two. Maybe you are trying to tell me something I don't want to deal with, or maybe you know something that I don't. Do tell, and then we can shift to better feelings."

It can be that simple. I can morph to being an observer while experiencing the fluctuation of moods and feelings, which makes all the difference. Negative voices are detrimental, much like the harsh vibes coming out of a bad roommate.

Journal writing helps a lot when I'm in transition or facing a dilemma. I am my own best friend, but it took me decades to get here. It is the ultimate positive experience of aging. Where was that voice during my thirties? Traveling the path to becoming a whole person often takes a lifetime; it's rare to arrive early.

I have figured out that pain and suffering is just another element to life. It surely makes you more compassionate to others. We are here on earth to experience the rainbow – good, bad, and indifferent – and then help others with their journey. It may sound like New Age pop psychology, but it's so true. And it's not new! The same philosophy has been embraced in nearly every religion for centuries.

I had always been so afraid of negative or dark feelings. That fear alone promotes anxiety. We are only as anxious as our hidden lies, so let it all come to the surface. I'd recommend that anyone and everyone practice the skill of sitting quietly while focusing on your breathing.

Yoga has been another life saver. I started yoga with an Israeli sage at our local JCC over ten years ago. Ell has a calming voice that takes a room full of regular middle-aged ladies through gentle yoga. You gently transition from one pose to another, almost in a meditative trance. It's not always beauty and tranquility with senior ladies. Some people do drift off and start snoring, and you will hear an occasional fart during group meditation. After that, no one can concentrate on their practice because everyone is wondering who invoked the spirit of the wind. If you can't find inner peace, find a laugh!

Sometimes (not in group meditation) I forget where I am as I drift in and out of sleep. Then I bring my focus back to my breathing so that relaxation doesn't put me to sleep. Whenever I start to get a wound-up monkey mind with racing thoughts (usually about my errands and chores), I return to my breathing practice. The deep, repetitive breathing raises my endorphins for the day. What could be more blissful? Then I make a beeline for Gelson's for an iced tea before I get on with my day.

Those simple pleasures during my week get me through the chaos of life and dealing with the news. I try not to actively listen to the political wars, hate, and senseless killings, but I can't live in a bubble. I read about the top five national news events each morning to make sure our world is still turning, and then I let it go for the rest of the day. And even at my age, I struggle to contain my screen time on the iPhone.

I believe in the power of therapy. Some people are on an intellectual and emotional plane that needs the support of a mentor or therapist. We need to know that there is nothing wrong with this. Life is hard, and I never judge one's pain and suffering.

Therapy for life tragedies and major changes can get you on the right path, along with the power of time. Time can sometimes heal all wounds but having another pillar of strength and wisdom surely eases the journey. For some, cognitive therapy partnered with judicious pharmaceutical medication can make a significant and profound difference in the quality of life. Therapy for me today is more about a mentor/mentee relationship than psychotherapy. My therapist and I share enlightening books and, from cortex to cortex, we examine the complexities of living and growing.

The most valuable thing I learned from the years of therapy is to gracefully accept the impermanence of life. Aging, the loss of loved ones, and our own demise are inevitable. Accept, and then devote your time to develop a full, enjoyable life. I've told my girls that when you see joy, jump on it and go for the gusto. It lifts a ton of bricks off my chest when I sweep away the angst of living. Many people don't want to discuss the profound issues, but it means they must live with the residue of fear. Remember, everyone always tells you that they are fine, regardless of how they are doing.

It can be very hard to face our demons, but if we persevere through our pain, we can get to the other side. And on days when life seems impossible, it is best to put the negative feelings in your suitcase and take it with you to handle later.

When I was teaching high school, I saw some students who struggled not just with academics, but with life. I instructed them to write a brief essay on the eight axioms to living a joyful poetic life, as described in Rainer Maria Rilke's philosophy. The exercise was both cathartic and enlightening; we followed up with an invigorating discussion. Later, the students presented their finished work in an essay to their parents at Thanksgiving. It was a chance to plant the seeds of discipline and meaning in the fertile minds of these young adults. The Los Angeles Times showcased this assignment, and my students were very pleased. Rilke's short list is a good set of rules for all of us:

- Be patient with ourselves and others
- Practice humility
- Trust our intuition
- Be personally responsible for our own inward discipline
- Learn about ourselves through solitude
- Concentrate through contemplation of life from our highest perspective
- Appreciate the beauty and good in nature and all things
- Live the poetic spirit every day

By now, you understand that I love tea for its flavor, for the ritual, and for medicinal purposes. Here is tea for aches and pains, arthritis, osteoarthritis, fibromyalgia, or anything else that hurts.

TURMERIC TEA

INGREDIENTS
- 1 tsp cinnamon and turmeric powder
- 1 tsp freshly grated ginger
- Pinch of nutmeg
- 1 1/2 cups of water
- Honey as needed
- Milk, nut milk, or cream

DIRECTIONS
- Simmer herbs and ginger in water for ten minutes, low heat
- Add honey and milk
- Enjoy with one chocolate square of your choice!

CHAPTER 13

ELEMENTS OF SIMPLICITY

"China tea, the scent of hyacinths, wood fires,
and bowls of violets — that is my mental picture
of an agreeable February afternoon."

— Constance Spry

Life can be comfortable with the simple pleasures of home. It is important to make your home your castle, no matter where you live or the size of your place. Two prime spots in any home are the bedroom and the kitchen.

My bed must be cozy and luxurious because I spend most of my evening hours there reading, writing, or streaming Netflix and Prime. My kitchen, naturally, is the place where I love to make delicious healthy meals. I have my old favorites, but I still read cookbooks and search food blogs for weekly ideas.

I live with our dog Cowboy and my husband of over forty years. David and I are very compatible with each other because we do our own thing at night. Cowboy, on the other hand, would never let me out of his sight. I have spoiled him, I know. He will refuse any food except fresh chicken with rice, and he sleeps with us. My husband walks him daily, and it is a good exercise for both.

I aim for simplicity with my clothes and accessories. My role model is my friend Lori. Despite her considerable wealth, she owns and wears just three pieces of jewelry: a small pair of gold circular stud earrings that her mother gave her, a simple watch, and a gold Cartier wedding band with a one-karat stone. I love that. If you added up all the junky jewelry that we buy over the years, three fine pieces would work just as well. I admire Lori's spartan taste and authenticity. Lori is also an educator devoted to developing programs for underprivileged children. She's the real deal.

Day to day, most people wear only twenty percent of their clothing, especially since the Covid-19 pandemic. I wore black leggings daily, a t-shirt (short or long according to the weather), and sneakers. I can barely go back to wearing regular pants with a tight waistband. My long sleeve cardigan was always with me. It became my uniform as well as an important signal of embracing a simpler way of living. I think I can boil it down to the twenty items of clothing that we really need:

1. A crisp, white shirt
2. T-shirts from the Gap: white, black, grey, blue
3. Blue jeans with stretch
4. Black slacks
5. Black blazer; buy a good but simple one
6. Black leggings
7. Khaki slacks and/or shorts
8. Bathing suit; one-piece with basic cover-up
9. Black button-down cardigan
10. Pull over cashmere sweater
11. Adidas jacket and matching pants
12. Sundress - midi

13. Black simple dress - Ralph Lauren
14. Straw hat, baseball cap hat
15. Jacket (one summer, one winter)
16. London Fog khaki raincoat with zipper lining
17. Puffer vest
18. Black skirt
19. Light weight white sweater for summer
20. Khaki sleeveless shell

To go with this lineup, a short list of accessories:

1. One shoulder bag, one tote, one evening bag
2. One pair of stud earrings and/or hoops (gold or silver)
3. One simple necklace and or pearl necklace
4. One band ring
5. Shoes - black flat, pump, sandal and/or wedge shoe

Most people spend a lot of time in their homes. It should be your place of comfort, peace, and beauty. Make your home your castle with some of these ten tips.

1. Bedrooms should be serene with a comfy plush bed and lots of pillows.
2. Duvet covers are easy to clean. The comforter should be thick and organic.
3. A beautiful throw displayed on the bed is nice to grab during cold nights.
4. A recliner chair in a corner is inviting to read a book or sip a hot cup of tea.
5. Meditation, journaling, reading, or listening to music can be enjoyed in any room.
6. Drapes or shades define the home's décor and finish a room.

7. Keep flowers everywhere in glass vases. Trader Joe's has inexpensive bouquets and plants.
8. Keep a supply of easy cookbooks to inspire healthy eating.
9. Design a reading corner for reading books and magazines or playing games and puzzles.
10. Area rugs make a room warm and centered.

Cabinets and pantry rooms should be fully stocked but not cluttered. Here are twenty essential staples to have on hand to make a meal in a jiffy. Purchase matching bins to sort the items.

1. Pasta, rice, and whole grains like faro
2. Oatmeal and cereals
3. Lentils, beans, and peas
4. Popcorn and corn chips
5. Nuts – all kinds
6. Olive oil and avocado oil
7. White flour, almond flour, and whole wheat flour
8. Sugar, honey, and maple syrup
9. Jams and jellies
10. Almond butter and/or peanut butter – organic
11. Cans of tuna, salmon, chicken, smoked oysters, and sardines
12. Salsa jars, olives, and salad dressings
13. Pumpkin puree
14. Protein bars
15. Water and soft drinks
16. Wine – red and white
17. Coffee and teas
18. Baking powder and baking soda
19. Spices
20. Chocolate – of course

You can shop on Wayfair, Amazon, IKEA or Target for inexpensive essentials and décor.

If there is a mantra for aging, it is "simplify." I was determined to declutter my house and garage in Newport Beach, and I worked on it for a couple of years. We had decades of stuff to donate or discard. For example, I don't anticipate that I will be entertaining more than eight people at a time. Yet, I had thirty-six crystal wine glasses and three sets of dishes. I gave away most of my multiple serving platters. Does anyone really need four cheese graters? Becoming organized makes me feel like I am in control and clearing out stuff generates new positive energy.

My husband was reluctant to part with his four tool sets in the garage. You might wonder if mechanical tools may be a surrogate for another "tool," but sometimes a cigar is just a cigar. Our garage was a disaster and the biggest challenge. Wires, old electronics, paint supplies, (he doesn't paint) and a boatload of Home Depot inventory had collected spiderwebs in the cabinets. David had multiple bins stacked up against the wall. I could see old Listerine bottles and expired products through the plastic bins. We had six staplers, masking tape holders, and dozens of boxes of paper clips.

I now crave simplicity and order. But where is the line between "simple and basic" and "grandma can't work the remote?" Recently I was gifted a Kindle, an Instapot, and a subscription to Audible. It was frustrating, even annoying, trying to figure it all out.

Cashless payment systems like Venmo and Zelle aren't in my comfort zone. Am I giving money or getting money? I once attempted to donate fifty dollars to a charity, but I accidentally typed an extra zero. My unintended $500 contribution was eventually corrected, but what a hassle. I miss writing checks! The endless hours of trying to set up auto-pay – does that mean

I crave the simple ways, or that I'm out of touch with modern technology?

At my age, the lips go white, the eyebrows thin, and the dull face needs some color. Yet I now wear minimal make-up: a tinted moisturizer, a combo lip-and-cheek stick, eyebrow pencil, brown lid shadow, and sometimes a bit of mascara. It takes five items and five minutes to put my face on so that people stop telling me that I look tired. I still get my hair colored and I do my own nails using a pale shade to disguise any chipping. I moisturize with Oil of Olay. That's it!

Despite some more recent use of normal looking people in TV and movies, our culture still celebrates good looks and toned bodies. Plastic surgery, once seen as a tool for the rich and desperate, has become common for even the very young. Magazines have more cosmetic procedure ads than any other content.

From my time in California, I feel that the residents are more health conscious there than in any other state. My lunch friends would often order skinless chicken with a steamed vegetable, leaving me feeling reckless and guilty when I ordered a personal pizza or French fries.

When I get hunger pangs, my instinct is to search the house for chocolate; I try to resist by first diverting to my own list of the twenty healthiest foods. Any of these healthy options might redirect your urges: beans, blueberries, broccoli, oatmeal, oranges, pumpkin seeds, salmon, basil, spinach, tea (black, white, or green), tomatoes, turkey, walnuts, yogurt, brown rice, yams, eggs, salad greens, lentils, and avocados.

We strive to be good, even great – but not perfect! I forgive myself for all these transgressions, and you should too: watching daytime television; eating milk chocolate instead of dark; drinking white wine instead of red wine; indulging in gluten-rich bagels with cream cheese; cursing the pram with twins blocking the aisles at Gelson's; drinking tap water at restaurants instead of their twenty-dollar bottled water.

Family and friends are essential at any stage of life, but I appreciate them more than ever. Having grandchildren has gone a long way to make up for the downside of aging. My daughter Ashlie and her husband Lou are raising two incredible children. I couldn't be prouder of their healthy and happy lifestyle. One axiom for parents is that "you're only as happy as your least happy child." When your kids are happy, healthy, and productive, it is the frosting on the banana cake.

THE BEST BANANA BREAD

INGREDIENTS
- 2 eggs
- 1/3 cup buttermilk
- 1/2 cup vegetable oil
- 1 cup mashed ripe bananas
- 1 cup white sugar
- 1/2 cup brown sugar
- 1 tsp vanilla
- 1 3/4 cup flour
- 1 tsp baking soda
- 1/2 tsp salt

DIRECTIONS
- Preheat oven to 325 degrees F; oil a 9 x 5 loaf pan
- In large bowl, whisk together eggs, buttermilk, and oil until well beaten
- Add in mashed bananas, both sugars, and vanilla. Mix well
- Sift in flour, baking soda, and salt. Mix but do not over mix
- Pour into greased loaf pan and bake for about one hour. Check doneness with a toothpick; ovens will vary

HEALTHY 3-INGREDIENT OATMEAL BANANA COOKIES

- Preheat oven to 350 F
- Line a cookie sheet with parchment paper
- Mix 3 overly ripe bananas, 1 1/2 cup oatmeal, and your choice of cinnamon, raisins, walnuts, and/or a few chocolate chips
- Form into balls, place on parchment
- Bake for 17 minutes

Both recipes are best enjoyed with lemon and ginger tea.

CHAPTER 14

CORONAVIRUS, POLITICS, AND ME

"The art of tea is a spiritual force for us to share."

— *Alexandra Stoddard*

In many ways, 2020 and 2021 are years to forget. The pernicious coronavirus was the stuff of science fiction until it mushroomed into a true-to-life disaster. During the first six months of quasi-lockdown (although I like to call it cocooning) with David and Cowboy, I often enjoyed the solitude. But as the pandemic dragged on, we began to feel a bit like caged animals. Given our ages, we are both high risk people who need to be careful.

In that same time frame, the brutal murder of George Floyd precipitated a movement throughout America with turmoil that felt like the unrest of the 1960s. Protesters, peaceful and violent, flooded our televisions daily as citizens felt that they had to choose a side: Black Lives Matter or Blue Lives Matter. But with age and wisdom, we know that it's rarely useful to see things as a choice of extreme views; don't forget the middle ground.

It was not that long ago when Republicans and Democrats would argue all day about conservative versus liberal positions and then go have a drink together (most famously, Ronald Reagan and Tip O'Neill). By 2020, the battle was more like creeping fascism and an attempted coup versus democracy. Even in Gelson's coffee bar, many were loudly proclaiming their political views; I tried to remain ambiguous/neutral for the sake of maintaining the camaraderie and my peaceful tea ritual.

It reminds me of my hula hoop "syndrome." When I was about six, my neighbor's father brought a dozen multi-colored hula hoops to a bunch of little girls in my neighborhood. Each girl called out the color of her choice: blue, yellow, pink, orange, green. I stood there with no answer and no choice of color. I didn't have a favorite color, and it made me feel odd.

My husband often has this dilemma when ordering food in a restaurant. He will look at me and ask me what I think he should eat. He too has the hula hoop syndrome. Whenever I can't decide on something, whether it's a pair of shoes or a paint color for my bedroom, I think of my hula-hoop syndrome.

I may not be able to choose a favorite color, but I do have some feelings on recent turbulent events. The more time you spend on the planet, the more cycles of behavior you see, and it helps put a perspective on things that others may be seeing for the first time.

Inhumanity has existed since Adam and Eve, or when the first human descended from the apes, or whatever starting point you choose. War, genocide, slavery, the Holocaust. Men can be evil. Men can be good.

It's silly to think that we can ban or "defund" the police, and it's not realistic to think that we need to support the police no matter what. Middle ground! There are good police and bad police. Most police forces could use better screening of applicants and certainly, more training is indicated. I wouldn't want to live without the police.

Education is surely integral to progress. It is a pressing need to improve and expand educational systems in America, starting with children under five years old. And specifically, early special education is imperative for children with learning difficulties, including autism. Good schooling should be augmented by accessible after school programs. We can recruit volunteers and college graduates for these programs, so valuable to working parents and their kids.

As a lifelong educator, I know the value of getting better trained (and better paid) teachers in our schools. There is so much disparity in opportunity, which of course leads to the social friction from disparate outcomes. Students in the USA have fallen behind other advanced nations in reading, math, and science. We need to focus on providing excellent schools for all children.

In essence, we need respect for humanity across the board, law and order, compassion for the other side, and tea to settle down.

I'd love to think that it will be one hundred years until the next global pandemic, just as it was for the time between the pandemic of 1918 (generally mislabeled as the Spanish flu) and covid. But one great lesson of this pandemic is that we need to be prepared, and we need ways to cope and to adjust.

I've found my own methodology for surviving pandemic conditions, and some of these may suit you too: bake healthy oatmeal cookies; break out your old cookbooks to make lovely dinners with wine and music; stay present in your garden or yard, drink in the sunshine; call one friend or relative a day (Facetime with a cocktail!) to stay connected to live people; drink tea in the afternoon and place flowers around the house; read an entertaining book or watch a cooking show; clean drawers, organize the garage, empty out closets; call an old friend, perhaps someone you knew in high school; watch old movies on TCM; walk your pet or borrow your neighbor's; play classical music throughout the house; help a neighbor from afar or a senior in your neighborhood; paint, write, sing, dance, create; turn off the news; stay grateful for all the good things in your life.

My hula-hoop syndrome also extends to religion and politics. I have friends who depend on their faith to get through the tough times. I grew up in a non-religious, non-political home. I am ambiguous with religion and sometimes with politics. Organized religion never worked for me. I was always the stranger in the house of worship. However, religion is a positive practice for many, and I encourage people to embrace their beliefs in times of darkness or despair. I do have my own vision of a higher power.

My life has been about learning lessons and meeting those challenges with acceptance. Mom always said, "What is, is." And I say, "Make your mess, learn from it, and help those in need."

Pausing helps when there are no visible answers. Sitting still and being quiet can bring on inner voices of wisdom. Just remember, if you take anything away from what I have learned over my lifetime, it is that we have the power. We have the choice to change our way of thinking. Always! Great writers, lecturers, teachers, and sages can give us the wisdom to change our thoughts.

Cognitive therapy asks us to be present, recognizing that the way we think about things affects how we feel emotionally. If you need help with this, find a professional. Build your serenity castle. Have a cup of tea, process the feelings, and then identify the free-floating anxiety. That can position you to take mental action and shift to a new understanding. Take that opportunity to sit quietly and evaluate.

My time on this earth has seen some difficult circumstances, including life-and-death experiences: the horrific MGM hotel fire, panic attacks, PTSD, infertility, miscarriages, financial challenges, health issues, and the loss of a child. There is an old saying that goes something like "If everyone laid their problems in the middle of a street for exchange, chances are each person would pick up their own problems and not someone else's." I'm not sure about that but I have been blessed in so many ways.

What I do know for certain is that if we persevere through life, we'll enjoy the most satisfaction between the bouts of hardship.

Here are *Lynda's Nine Maxims for Living Well*:

1. Regardless of your childhood, you have gaps to fill. You must discover and become the voice of your own mother and father within. Everyone has the capability.

2. Self-compassion is the answer to getting through any struggle. It is the most important "aha moment." You can't get it from reading a book. It is your own wake-up call and commitment.

3. We all have resilience. We all have grit. It comes down to using that muscle. There will always be a fork in the road. You get to choose. You do, you get to choose.

4. Your body is your temple. What you eat and drink will determine your life span.

5. Family and friends are the keys to a full house, even if you live alone. There are clubs to join. Add pets to your life and you will never be lonely.

6. Stay present! Past and future thoughts should only be ten percent of your day. Meditate, practice yoga, or walk with nature to feed your soul. Make some nourishing soup.

7. Mourning and loss of any kind need to be put in a separate room in your home. It's okay to visit and journal about it but then put it away. Plan your day.

8. Learn, educate, grow, and stay fresh. Experience something new, take up a hobby. Find your gifts, talents, and hobbies and then share. Volunteer!

9. The simple pleasure of tea, hot or iced, is part of my ritual for experiencing the present moment. It is an understated pleasure that can bring one to a peaceful state of being at any time or any place. Laugh, find humor. Life can be good. Very good, in fact, so drink tea!

HEALTHFUL OATMEAL COOKIES

INGREDIENTS
- 3/4 cup butter
- 1 cup brown sugar
- 1 egg
- 1/4 cup water
- 1 tsp vanilla
- 2 1/2 cups oatmeal
- 3/4 cup flour or almond flour
- 1/2 tsp salt
- 1/2 tsp baking soda
- Handful of chopped pecans (optional)

DIRECTIONS
- Preheat oven to 350 degrees F
- Combine the wet ingredients together and then add to the dry; mix well and then add nuts
- Place 1/4 cup dough per cookie on greased baking sheet
- Bake 12-15 minutes
- Makes 18 cookies
- Serve with mint and ginger tea

CHAPTER 15

THE COWGIRL FROM NEWPORT BEACH

"Cowgirl boots are a cowgirl's attire
and a city girl's desire."

—Rachel Lynn

As much as I have loved my iced tea jaunts to various Gelson's throughout Southern California over the decades, not long ago I was confronted with fresh circumstances that compelled us to leave California and make a new life. What could take me away from this sunny paradise? Nothing, except for one thing – grandchildren!

Not long before the pandemic reached America, my daughter and her family moved to Lakeway, an Austin suburb, for her husband's family business. Austin, the capital city, is the hippest and most liberal city in the big red state of Texas. It's known for its cool vibe, the University of Texas and its Longhorn teams, and great restaurants. Perhaps most importantly, Austin is recognized as the live music capital of the USA. Lakeway is just 10 minutes from Willie Nelson's home, Luck Ranch.

Austin has attracted a lot of high-tech companies, like Apple and Tesla, due to a friendly business environment and a supply of well-educated workers. Even more tech workers are moving to Austin due to the expanding job opportunities, the excellent schools, and the lack of a state income tax. It must be said, though, that some long-time Texans don't welcome the California newcomers because they're driving up the price of real estate.

We visited my daughter's family several times in Texas, but then we were restricted from seeing them when covid was rampaging. It was tortuous to leave Newport Beach, Gelson's, and all the great memories, but we sold our California house and moved to the Austin suburbs. Perhaps it was an omen that we had chosen the name "Cowboy" for our Bichon pup over a decade earlier.

Our arrival to our new home was coincidental to one of the worst snow and ice storms that Austin had ever seen. For three days in a row, the daily high temperature did not exceed 5 degrees Fahrenheit! This is nothing in Chicago, but Central Texas is not at all prepared for such conditions. Austin is further south than San Diego, further south than Phoenix, further south than Jacksonville. The arid landscape is dotted with cactus and palm trees.

Systems aren't built to withstand a deep freeze, and homeowners aren't experienced in simple things like insulating outdoor hose spigots or leaving an inside faucet dripping to prevent frozen pipes. The entire region was unprepared for this storm. There are practically no snowplows; hence, homes and businesses that are heated by propane could get no deliveries. Many around us lost power, lost water, and experienced broken water pipes and/or broken pumps for well water. Plumbers were quickly booked out for weeks.

This storm was a true disaster and was designated so by the federal government. Rolling blackouts continued in our immediate area, but we were fortunate not to lose our power. In our Austin suburb, we're fortunate to be served by a well-run electric co-op; the rest of the state was not so lucky, and the failure of the Texas-only power grid and the large utilities made national news.

This was a test. California certainly has its problems with earthquake and fires, but this was a shock to us. We experienced the 1994 earthquake while we lived in Calabasas, and we sustained $75,000 of damage. We also were evacuated from our house a couple of times due to the fires. Beyond the inability to cope with a freak winter storm, this part of Texas can also see floods and tornados.

To add to those big threats, I also have a fear of snakes and these serpents are ubiquitous, especially during the hot summer. The locals say that 90% of the snakes here are not venomous, but we have rattlers and copperheads and cottonmouth snakes. And it's common to find a scorpion in the house! I questioned the wisdom of leaving California for Texas.

Well, I questioned the move for maybe five minutes. But every time I look into the blue eyes of my beautiful grandchildren Ryder and Ruby, my heart sinks and I know we did the right thing. Family really is everything. We're in a lovely town called Lakeway, named for nearby Lake Travis. We're just 30 minutes from all the excitement of downtown Austin, but it's like pioneer land to our immediate west, with long stretches of sparse two-lane roads that crisscross the cattle ranches.

Here in Lakeway we have an ideal mix of urban and rural; we all love the surrounding wonders of nature, lakefront, hiking trails, deer and other wildlife, and clean living. Austin is surely growing on me.

My Buddhist mentor has been guiding me through this transition. I zoom with her as needed. Some days I love the change, and other days I am like Dorothy lamenting "this isn't Kansas, Toto." No, and this isn't Newport Beach either. Still, I don't miss it as much as I thought I would because there is so much beauty here.

Moving, especially at my age, was a major stress even though it is a happy new chapter in our lives. I had to pause and search for my inner home. Lewis Carroll said it best, "If you don't know where you are going, any road will get you there."

I do miss my friends, my decades-long acquaintances, the ocean, and of course Gelson's. But I found a new joint, *The Austin Tea Exchange.* I immediately liked Michael, the owner, on my first visit to his unique tea cafe. I learned that he is a native New Yorker, and our big-city backgrounds helped us to connect immediately. His teas are fresh-brewed every day, hot and cold. I enjoy the muffins, croissants, almond sweet rolls, and other tempting delicacies to have with my tea. With seating both inside and outside, it's a great meeting place for a very cosmopolitan crowd.

Lakeway is far enough west to be in Texas Hill Country, and it is a healthy environment to raise children. The outdoor sports and activities are outstanding, as we appreciate the down-to-earth people. We're so glad we decided to be with our family; John Lennon may have said it best, "Love is all you need."

Central Texas has very hot (but dry) weather during the summer, and it can be oppressive. However, the culture, the people, and the music in Austin have been a welcome change. I was pleasantly surprised to learn that it is sunny almost every day, and the air quality is excellent. Fall and winter have clean, crisp air with moderate temperatures in the 50s.

The University of Texas is downtown and naturally draws a lot of highly educated people from all over the world. This clean city with multiple lakes feels like a petite San Francisco without the fog. Still, it will take time to assimilate to the area.

Austin is becoming more cosmopolitan due to the billion-dollar companies relocating here, along with all the people moving to Texas from Illinois, California, and the east coast. Austin has people from all walks of life, and I welcome that. However, when I saw a man in a local restaurant lick all ten fingers after he devoured his chicken-fried steak with mashed potatoes and gravy, I almost threw up.

Every home has a pickup truck in the driveway. It's a practical necessity for the working men and women, especially the Texas natives. But it seems more like a branding exercise for these newly imported Texans, who motor to the Starbucks and the gym in their Ford F150 and Dodge Ram trucks. Compared to my time in Southern California, the men here sport a more rugged appearance. To go with the trucks, most homes have one or more guns. But this is part of living in Texas.

I have a half-dozen amazing girlfriends whom I have known for decades; they are just a phone call or text away. I treasure my women friends for their level of emotional insight and willingness to share, something I rarely find in men. Men love their careers, sports, cars, food and of course sex. Many men have intellectual firepower in science, math, business, law, medicine, mechanics, and how the world runs, but they are not as attuned to spiritual awakening, fashion, hormonal mood swings, or the need to gossip. Men don't talk about their "aha moments."

Men often anchor women, although I have seen reversed roles where the woman is clearly the alpha. However, women can also anchor men with their organization skills, concentration (most men I've known seem to have attention deficits), and scheduling appointments. We are often the psychologist, nurse, maid, cook, teacher, and house managers. But somehow it all works out.

Women will always have a sisterhood, but age and wisdom teach us to beware of frenemies! I define frenemy as a person with whom one is friendly on the surface, despite a fundamental dislike or rivalry. Sometimes we need to examine the value of a "friend" when any of these red flags overshadow the relationship:

- She makes you feel "less than" with money or power
- She is a gossip queen
- She's inauthentic, materialistic, and mean-spirited
- She displays envy and a need to compete or compare
- She judges you when you share your vulnerability
- She doesn't stick with you for the good, the bad, and the ugly
- She makes it feel like you are Ethel and she is Lucy
- She subjects you to her temper tantrums
- She is rigid and intolerant in religious and political views
- She drags you down with constant negativity
- She weighs less than you (just kidding)

My sister is my best friend. If you have one, you are lucky. Yes, there has been some rivalry, but that was long ago. We have been together through our family secrets, aging parents, obnoxious relatives, decades of experiences, and best of all, laughing until it hurts. I love the family, friends, and peeps who have filled my life's tapestry. We have shared so much over the years, and it makes me a very rich woman.

Making friends at my age can be challenging. Most people have made their friends from their children's friends and their families as they were growing up. That's okay, because I have my interest, hobbies, business, and of course my family. Hubby and I are often a twosome.

I don't avoid big social groups or parties, but I don't need them either. Frequently, the small talk makes me uncomfortable. I once encountered a woman who, within the first ten minutes of our conversation, asked me if I still had my uterus. I do enjoy the company of my small groups of peeps. I also enjoy the one-on-one interaction, particularly with my closest friends.

My new neighborhood has a community center with yoga classes, book clubs, bridge, and other group activities. While some embrace every organized opportunity to socialize, I no longer feel that compulsion (although I do go to the yoga classes). I can be perfectly happy to go to the lakeside and drink in nature's beauty. Top that off with my home-made iced tea, and I'm in my happy placc.

TEXAS ICED TEA

INGREDIENTS
- Brewed Earl Grey iced tea
- Tequila

DIRECTIONS
- Mix equal parts tequila and iced tea
- Pour over ice and stir
- Serve cold in a highball glass and enjoy!

CHAPTER 16

AFTERNOON TEA PARTY

"Tea washes the spirit"
— *Chinese proverb*

There is nothing like having my gal friends over for a tea party. It is simpler than you think. Set the tone for a wonderful afternoon with flowers throughout the home and a few teapots. You don't need a three-tier server to display your pastries or scones, but it's a nice touch. Alternatively, form a pedestal by placing a bowl upside down on the table and draping a beautiful linen napkin over the bowl. Then you can put a plate of your goodies on the bowl to give some height to your presentation.

You can use a variety of plates for serving around a centerpiece like a vase of fresh flowers. Your teacups and teapots can be on your kitchen counter or a side table. More flowers add to the beauty of your presentation. This is the time to use your linens, centerpieces, tableware, and more flowers while setting the mood with color schemes and background music (classical or soft jazz). To accompany your teas, prepare a variety of light

offerings like scones, dainty desserts, and assorted finger sandwiches (four to five sandwiches per person). Homemade or store-
bought pastries will work fine.

I love chicken, crab, tuna, and salmon for making tea sandwiches. Simple mayonnaise and celery can be added to the mix.
Many people are quite particular about their mayo; I am devoted
to Hellman's (or Best Foods – same mayo, different name). Folks
here in Texas and much of the south are gaga about Duke's mayonnaise, and another fun choice is Kewpie, the Japanese mayo
that has MSG in it. If you want to shave some calories, you can
mix the mayo with Greek yogurt.

AFTERNOON TEA

Here's what typically goes into tea sandwiches. Use your imagination as you assemble the breads, fillings, and condiments.

Breads
Pepperidge Farm white thin sliced bread (use round cookie cutters to make circular bread), petite croissants, small square rye thins, mini potato buns

Fillings
Ham, chicken, tuna, crab, hard boiled eggs, salmon lox, cucumbers, radishes,
cheese (mozzarella, brie, Swiss, Havarti, goat, feta), prosciutto, tomatoes, apples, avocados

Condiments
Cream cheese, peppered jelly, horseradish, honey, lemon curd, jams and jellies, basil leaves, mustard (yellow, brown, spicy, stone ground)

Teas (make it simple)
Black, green, white, grey earl, jasmine, oolong, or any of your choice

A large bowl of fresh berries (blueberries, strawberries, raspberries, blackberries, gooseberries) or a bowl of potato salad can round out your menu.

MAMA Z'S POTATO SALAD

INGREDIENTS
- 8 white potatoes (whole, peeled)
- 1 white onion, diced
- 2 stalks of celery, diced
- 2 tbsp vinegar
- 1 tbsp sugar
- 1/2 cup Best Foods or Hellman's Mayonnaise
- Celery salt, pepper, and salt, to taste
- 1 tbsp chopped parsley
- 1 tbsp sweet paprika

DIRECTIONS
- Boil potatoes for 25 minutes or until tender
- Cut potatoes into small chunks
- Combine with celery and onion in a large bowl
- Add spices/sugar/vinegar
- Marinate and refrigerate at least 2 hours
- Add cold mayonnaise, mix
- Sprinkle with parsley and sweet paprika. Enjoy!

MY FAVORITE BOOKS

"There are few things nicer than sitting up in bed, drinking strong tea, and reading."

— *Alan Clark*

FICTION

1. To Kill a Mockingbird - Harper Lee

2. The Lord of the Flies - William Golding

3. Almost Paradise - Susan Isaacs

4. The Great Gatsby - F. Scott Fitzgerald

5. Prince of Tides - Pat Convoy

6. She's Come Undone - Wally Lamb

7. East of Eden - John Steinbeck

8. Catcher in the Rye - J. D. Salinger

9. Sophies Choice - William Styron

10. Water for Elephants - Sara Gruen

11. Goldengrove - Francine Prose

12. Pilgrim at Tinker Creek - Annie Dillard

13. The Four Winds - Kristin Hannah

14. The Fault in Our Stars - John Green

NON-FICTION

1. The Road Less Traveled - M. Scott Peck

2. Flow - Mihaly Csikszentmihalyi

3. Creativity - Mihaly Csikszentmihalyi

4. The Four Agreements - Don Miguel Ruiz

5. Man's Search for Meaning - Viktor E. Frankl

6. The Art of Aging - Sherwin B. Nuland

7. Brief Answers to the Big Questions - Stephen Hawking

8. The Denial of Death - Ernest Becker

9. A Path with Heart - Jack Kornfield

10. When Things Fall Apart - Pema Chodron

11. The Wisdom of No Escape - Pema Chodron

12. Simple Abundance - Sarah Ban Breathnach

13. The Tibetan Book of Living and Dying - Sogyal Rinpoche

14. The Untethered Soul - Michael A. Singer

15. The Book of Awakening - Mark Nepo

16. Finding Inner Courage - Mark Nepo

17. The Happiness Makeover - M.J. Ryan

18. A New Earth - Eckart Tolle

19. The Drama of the Gifted Child - Alice Miller

20. Too Soon Old, Too Late Smart - Gordon Livingston M.D

21. And Never Stop Dancing - Gordon Livingston M.D.

22. Living the Simple Life - Elaine St. James

23. The Art of Living - Epictetus

24. The World According to Mister Rogers - Fred Rogers

25. Dancing With Life - Phillip Moffitt

26. Yes to Life - Viktor E. Frankl

27. This Messy Magnificent Life - Geneen Roth

28. Women, Food, and God - Geneen Roth

29. The Blessing of a Skinned Knee - Wendy Mogel

30. Ten Ways to Awaken the Wise Heart: A Photographic Journey – Karen K. Redding PHD

BIOGRAPHIES and MEMOIRS

1. Eat, Pray, Love - Elizabeth Gilbert

2. Maybe You Should Talk to Someone - Lori Gottlieb

3. The Color of Water - James McBride

4. The Year of Magical Thinking - Joan Didion

5. Teacher Man - Frank McCourt

6. Rewrite: A Memoir - Neil Simon

7. The Choice - Edith Eva Eger

8. Throw Me the Rope: A Memoir on Loving Lauren – Lynda Zussman

WRITING

1. On Writing: A Memoir of the Craft - Stephen King

2. Writing Down the Bones - Natalie Goldberg

3. Screenplay - Syd Field

4. On Writing Well - William Zinsser

5. Bird by Bird - Anne Lamott

6. The Memoir Project - Marion Roach Smith

7. The Art of the Memoir - Mary Karr

8. Writing the Memoir - Judith Barrington

COOKBOOKS

1. Food to Live By - Myra Goodman

2. The Eat Clean Diet and Cookbook - Tosca Reno

3. Sonoma Diet Cookbook - Dr. Connie Guttersen

4. The Healthy Mind - Rebecca Katz

5. Cravings - Chrissy Teigen

6. Skinny Taste - Gina Homolka

7. Make It Healthy - Wolfgang Puck

8. Fast and Easy - Lisa Lillian

9. Plenty - Yotam Bholenghi

10. I Like You - Amy Sedaris

11. Weight Watchers Under 20: 200 Delicious Dishes in 20 Minutes or Less

12. Weight Watchers Power Food Cookbook

TEA

1. Afternoon Tea at Home - Will Torrent

2. The Book of Tea - Okakura Kakuzo

3. The Art of Teas: Recipes and Rituals - Jordon Marxer

4. The Tea Enthusiast's Handbook: A Guide to Enjoy the World's Best Teas - Mary Lou Heiss and Robert J. Heiss

5. A Social History of Teas: Tea's Influence on Commerce, Culture and Community - Jane Pettigrew and Bruce Richardson

6. The Tea Book: Experience the World's Finest Teas, Qualities, Infusions, Rituals, Recipes - Linda Gaylard

7. A History of Tea: The Life and Times of the World's Favorite Beverage - Laura C. Martin

Acknowledgements

This book has been a labor of love for the last decade, and I could not have made it to the finish line without the astute professional editorial skills of Martin Frappolli.

I also want to give a shout-out to the superior supermarket, Gelson's, for being my second home with incredible hard-working employees. There is no other market like it, and it has the best iced tea in the world. The coffee bar also has a tribe of people to whom I am grateful for being part of the daily community.

I have tremendous gratitude for my teacher and mentor, Karen K. Redding, for her wisdom, knowledge, and compassion during my darkest days. My spiritual growth and awakening grew each day while Karen walked with me through the rabbit hole.

I have so many people to thank for their support including my Peeps; Susan B., Kathy D., Trudy F., Viki I., Judi L., Tami Z., and my Newport Beach Peeps of twenty years; Lori C., Lorraine L., and Kelli N. We were the troublemakers at our monthly restaurant outings. You simply can't replace decades of true friendships with these amazing women. We have shared births, birthdays, marriages, illnesses, deaths, holidays, and iced tea meetups with compassion, joy, and gusto. I also want to thank my siblings, Judy and Roger, for keeping me out of trouble.

I am most grateful and proud of my two amazing daughters, Lauren and Ashlie, for also being my teachers in life, surfing the waves of parenting. I will do better and be better each day. I also give thanks for my son-in-law, Lou (Ashlie's hubby) and my shining stars, Ryder and Ruby.

Family is everything. You make every day a gift. And lastly, to my husband, David, the keeper of my heart and soul. Our history and memories can never be erased. Let's make new ones.